Maurice Procter and The Murder Room

›› This title is part of The Murder Room, our series dedicated to making available out-of-print or hard-to-find titles by classic crime writers.

Crime fiction has always held up a mirror to society. The Victorians were fascinated by sensational murder and the emerging science of detection; now we are obsessed with the forensic detail of violent death. And no other genre has so captivated and enthralled readers.

Vast troves of classic crime writing have for a long time been unavailable to all but the most dedicated frequenters of second-hand bookshops. The advent of digital publishing means that we are now able to bring you the backlists of a huge range of titles by classic and contemporary crime writers, some of which have been out of print for decades.

From the genteel amateur private eyes of the Golden Age and the femmes fatales of pulp fiction, to the morally ambiguous hard-boiled detectives of mid twentieth-century America and their descendants who walk our twenty-first century streets, The Murder Room has it all. ››

The Murder Room
Where Criminal Minds Meet

themurderroom.com

Maurice Procter 1906–1973

Born in Nelson, Lancashire, Maurice Procter attended the local grammar school and ran away to join the army at the age of fifteen. In 1927 he joined the police in Yorkshire and served in the force for nineteen years before his writing was published and he was able to write full-time. He was credited with an ability to write exciting stories while using his experience to create authentic detail. His procedural novels are set in Granchester, a fictional 1950s Manchester, and he is best known for his series characters, Detective Superintendent Philip Hunter and DCI Harry Martineau. Throughout his career, Procter's novels increased in popularity in both the UK and the US, and in 1960 *Hell is a City* was made into a film starring Stanley Baker and Billie Whitelaw. Procter was married to Winifred, and they had one child, Noel.

Philip Hunter

The Chief Inspector's Statement (1951)
   aka *The Pennycross Murders*
I Will Speak Daggers (1956)
   aka *The Ripper*

Chief Inspector Martineau

Hell is a City (1954)
   aka *Somewhere in This City*
The Midnight Plumber (1957)
Man in Ambush (1958)
Killer at Large (1959)

Devil's Due (1960)

The Devil Was Handsome (1961)

A Body to Spare (1962)

Moonlight Flitting (1963)
    aka *The Graveyard Rolls*

Two Men in Twenty (1964)

Homicide Blonde (1965)
    aka *Death has a Shadow*

His Weight in Gold (1966)

Rogue Running (1966)

Exercise Hoodwink (1967)

Hideaway (1968)

Standalone Novels

Each Man's Destiny (1947)

No Proud Chivalry (1947)

The End of the Street (1949)

Hurry the Darkness (1952)

Rich is the Treasure (1952)
    aka *Diamond Wizard*

The Pub Crawler (1956)

Three at the Angel (1958)

The Spearhead Death (1960)

Devil in Moonlight (1962)

The Dog Man (1969)

Devil's Due

Maurice Procter

An Orion book

Copyright © Maurice Procter 1960

The right of Maurice Procter to be identified as the author of this work
has been asserted in accordance with the Copyright, Designs and Patents
Act 1988.

This edition published by
The Orion Publishing Group Ltd
Orion House
5 Upper St Martin's Lane
London WC2H 9EA

An Hachette UK company
A CIP catalogue record for this book is available from the British Library

ISBN 978 1 4719 0271 0

www.orionbooks.co.uk

I

'THIS is going to be a real comic job,' Detective Chief Inspector Martineau said bitterly, as he looked at the two bodies on the ground. 'Nobody is going to come shouting the odds about these characters.'

The bodies had been men in their early thirties, above medium height and strongly built. Their clothes were good, but in style and hue not quite in good taste. Both men had been shot. Each of them still had a short, leather-covered club attached to his right wrist by a thong. They were lying some eight yards apart.

The police surgeon of the division was on his knees beside one of the bodies. He stood up and turned to Martineau. 'This one has had his head battered and his knuckles rapped, but not seriously,' he said. 'I think we'll find that bullets were the cause of death in both cases. Do you know this fellow?'

'Bert Kaplan,' the policeman growled, looking down at the body without pity. 'And the other one is Joe Ray. A couple of deadlegs.'

'Dead is the word,' said the doctor as he turned away. 'I'll see them later.'

Martineau stood watching his subordinates doing routine work with cameras and tape measures. He was a big, strong man, one of the most formidable of a thousand big men in the Granchester police. He wore a good suit of darkish grey, and, perplexed, he had pushed his hat to the back of his head. A sodium light overhead made his strong, not un-handsome face seem more than usually forbidding, and it showed his hair to be so blond that the grey in it could hardly be discerned even in daylight.

He looked up and down the wide, brightly-lit street,

1

which was deserted except for the group of detectives, and empty of traffic except for police cars. He looked at the second-rate shops with the glimmering windows of dingy offices above them. He thought of the little side streets which were so busy in the daytime, with offices, workshops, warehouses and small factories all higgledy-piggledy, solid businesses and struggling, shaky concerns mixed up anyhow. The side streets would be excellent avenues of escape for a slinking murderer who knew his way, with not a soul to see him go, and no residents to be awakened by the sound of his shots. A real comic job.

Detective Sergeant Devery approached. He was as tall as the chief inspector, but younger and slimmer. A cruiser-weight. It had been said in the past, by men since proved to be wrong, that Devery was much too handsome to make a good policeman.

'Well, sir,' he asked. 'Do we go and do the obvious?'

'See Costello, you mean? He'll be having a party with a popsie.'

'While somebody strews the streets with the bodies of his boys?'

'I'm betting he doesn't know about this do yet. If I could get it quick, I'd like to have something to work on when I talk to him.'

They were joined by the motor patrol officer who had discovered the bodies. 'Headquarters would like to speak to you, sir,' he said to Martineau.

The detective went to sit in the car. He announced himself. 'Yes, sir, one moment,' said the disembodied voice of Headquarters. Then: 'Here it is. A phone call reporting the shooting in Burleigh Street. At twelve fifty-seven.'

'One of our own men found the bodies at twelve forty-three.'

'That is so, sir. I asked this man why he hadn't reported the matter sooner, and he said that he hadn't had the time.'

'Oh, he did, did he? What's his name?'

'He declined to give name or address, sir.'

'Mmmm. Where was he calling from?'

'He refused to say. I made every effort to elicit the information.'

'A public telephone box?'

'Yes sir. I heard him press Button A.'

'What did he give you?'

'The time of the shooting, for a start. He said: "Twelve-thirty, as near as dammit".'

'That's about right according to the vet. What else?'

'He claimed to be an eye-witness. Briefly, sir, he said he saw two men chasing another man along Burleigh Street. The man who was being chased was carrying a brown fibre suitcase. When the others caught up with him he turned and shot them, and ran away. The witness said that it looked like a case of justifiable homicide.'

'A what?'

'A case of justifiable homicide.'

'He used those actual words?'

'Yes, sir. I asked how he knew that the suitcase was of fibre, and not leather. He did not reply immediately, then he said: "I'm sure it was fibre". This is his description of the man with the gun: "A man in his twenties, of medium height, slim but nicely built, rather a lot of dark hair, dark trousers, a jerkin or jacket which looked like brown leather, probably crêpe-soled shoes because he made no sound when he was running, no hat".'

'Well, that's something if it's true. How did it seem to you?'

'Hard to say, sir. He might be our man, throwing pepper at us.'

'Only too likely. Anyway, I suppose you've put out the word on it?'

'Yes. I kept asking the man questions, trying to detain him in the box till I could have him picked up, but he wouldn't wear it. He hung up on me.'

'Too bad. You did very well. This number to stand by,' said Martineau, then he turned and spoke through the open window of the car to Devery: 'So we've got a suspect, we hope.'

3

The sergeant listened to the description of the young man in the leather jacket. 'Never heard of him,' he said.

'Me neither,' the senior man said. 'Leather jacket. He won't be wearing it any more.'

'A medium sized lad with a lot of dark hair. There's a million of 'em.'

'I'm afraid so,' Martineau sighed. 'Come along, let's go see Costello.'

Dixie Costello lived in the middle of the town, in a flat above a restaurant he owned. It was a good restaurant, and a luxurious flat. When Martineau and Devery arrived there at twenty-five minutes past one, Costello's white Rolls-Royce was standing outside his private entrance. There were lights in several rooms of the flat, and there was music too. Somebody was thumping a piano with verve, vigour and ability.

Martineau pressed the bell button. He received no answer. He waited until the pianist came to the end of a popular chorus, then he pressed the bell insistently. Almost immediately the curtains were drawn back from a window, and Costello appeared. He opened the window, and looked down.

'Who's there?' he demanded. 'Whaddyer want?'

'Police,' Martineau replied. 'A word with you, Dixie.'

Costello was disgusted. 'Coppers at this time of night! Come and see me in the morning.'

'We'll see you now. It's important.'

'It couldn't be. What's it about?'

'Do you want me to shout it out?'

'You can if you like. I've got nothing to hide. But wait a minute, I'll let you in.'

The policemen waited. 'He seems half cut to me,' Devery murmured.

'Yes,' his companion agreed. 'But half cut he's smarter than most fellows when they're cold sober.'

The street door was opened by a burly man of forty or so. He had a face which was both tough and sly. He was Ned Higgs, Costello's right-hand man for many years.

'Evening, Inspector,' he said with a grin.

'Lead on, or get out of the way,' Martineau growled.

The grin remained on the face of Higgs. 'Dearie me, he's cross tonight,' he mocked as the callers followed him up the stairs.

They entered a large room with furnishings which gave the impression of comfort and careless luxury. The doors of a well-filled liquor cabinet stood wide open. The air was heavy with the odour of cigar smoke.

The girl who had been punishing the baby grand now reclined with an elbow upon it, and beside the elbow there was a spirit glass which had been generously filled. She was a tall, shapely redhead typical of Costello's taste, and though she was very young she obviously was not recently from a convent, or any other ladies' seminary. Her dress indicated that she had some taste but not much money. Therefore, it appeared, Dixie was not yet buying her clothes. She was a new girl and not yet a kept woman.

Apparently, as far as she was concerned, the party was not spoiled by the arrival of two policemen. She smiled at them with muzzy alcoholic friendliness.

Martineau glanced at the girl, nodded to Dixie, and turned to look at Higgs. The man's presence in the flat at that time of night had some significance, he was sure. Higgs was not there for social reasons, not when Dixie had a new girl for company.

'Are you the chaperone?' he asked drily. 'Or are you waiting for news?'

'News of what?' Dixie demanded.

'News of success, of course. Good news.'

'We're always ready for good news, but we've never known a copper ever bring any.'

'I hope that will always be true as far as you're concerned, Dixie. But of course you weren't waiting for the police, were you? You were waiting to hear how Kaplan and Ray had managed tonight.'

'Bert and Joey? What they been up to?' Dixie asked with just the right touch of nonchalant interest.

Martineau was nonchalant too. He very carefully concealed his growing excitement. There had been no tremor in Dixie's voice, but he had turned pale. Something had happened to make Dixie Costello turn pale!

The detective studied him, seeing a broad but compactly built man of middle height; strong and obviously formidable. He was about the same age as Higgs but much better looking, and recently – since an increasing amount of legitimate business had put him occasionally into the company of men of breeding – he had learned to conceal some of his ineradicable vulgarity. Nowadays the clothes he wore were quietly elegant, and diamonds no longer flashed on his fingers and his tie. His rasping voice no longer needed to carry the unspoken threat of razor and knuckle-duster. A shadowy authority had been his for a long time now, and an air of command seemed to be natural to him. He looked all right, the detective thought. He looked all right considering that he was a man who would conspire to any villainy to increase his wealth.

Martineau realized that he had prodded his man in a place where it hurt. The murder of two of his followers? That was something which might make him angry and vengeful: it would not make him lose colour. If he had had a hand in the killings, he might be perturbed if he thought that the police had evidence against him. But he would have to hear the evidence, and pretty conclusive evidence at that, before the ruddy glow of health and whisky faded from his cheeks. So what could it be? What could make Dixie Costello go white in a night? Material loss? Ah yes!

Dixie had received a hint that the police had made contact somewhere with Kaplan and Ray. That had upset him. If he did not know that the two men were dead, he probably had reason to think that they were under arrest, and that their arrest involved him in a heavy material loss. Which meant that he thought the police now had something which he considered to be his, but which he could not or dared not legally claim. Drugs? Jewels? Money? Stolen property in some form?

Something which could be carried in a fibre suitcase?

If Headquarters' anonymous informant was telling the truth, Dixie's men had been shot while trying to rob somebody. In all probability they had been acting under Dixie's orders. Not knowing that they had been killed, and assuming that they were under arrest, Dixie would suppose that they had been caught in the act of robbery. Would the mere thought of that make him turn pale, even if the intended booty had been extremely valuable? Martineau decided that it would not affect him at all. Dixie was a gambler. Heavy losses might make him look sick, but failure to win the other fellow's money would not.

Putting the thing the other way round, if Kaplan and Ray had been carrying something valuable, and the mere notion that the police had picked them up turned Dixie white, then the something would be stolen property, which Dixie would regard as his own as soon as it came into his possession. Its loss would be a real loss to him. So it could be that Mr. Anonymous had shot and robbed Kaplan and Ray, and was now for some reason of his own trying to sell the police a revised version of the crime. Mr. Anonymous might be a thief, a liar, and a murderer.

So it seemed, but it was only a theory. And as a theory it had one great weakness. The weakness was in the fact itself, if it was a fact. Two of Dixie Costello's men had been robbed of some of Dixie's property. That was hard to believe. Dixie was in the habit of managing things better than that.

'What were Kaplan and Ray doing for you tonight?' Martineau asked, and then he immediately realized that he had made a mistake. Dixie's colour returned. If the police did not know what Kaplan and Ray had been doing, then everything might yet be all right for Dixie.

'They weren't doing anything for me,' he replied. 'If they've got theirselves locked up, it's their own funeral.'

'How right you are. Have you had any new recruits to your mob lately?'

'No. Things are quiet. And I don't like that talk about a mob. All my business is above board.'

'Oh sure. Haven't you had any young fellow hanging around, hoping for a job?'

'That happens all the time. Kids hang around.'

'I don't mean all the time. I mean in the last week or two.'

'Well, I can't bring anybody to mind.'

'You might, when I tell you what it's all about.'

'I'm waiting for that. I thought I was going to have to wait all night.'

'Kaplan and Ray are dead.'

There was a small, meaningless cry from the girl. That was all. The faces of Costello and Higgs were so set in guarded immobility that they seemed not to have heard. There was silence, and then Martineau said drily: 'An expression of sympathy is customary.'

Dixie shrugged. 'What happened?' he asked quietly.

'They were shot. In Burleigh Street. They both had knobkerries in their hands when they were found. That could have been arranged by the man who shot them, of course.'

Dixie nodded. 'Sure, a fake.'

'Now will you tell me what they were doing for you?'

'They weren't doing anything for me. I've already told you that.'

'You can tell me again, and I still won't believe you. Give me the truth.'

Dixie looked up to heaven, or at least to the ceiling, as if he would find patience there. He had taken his shocks and recovered his usual hard composure. He asked: 'Any idea who did it?'

'I was hoping you might tell me.'

'How would I know? You're supposed to be the detective, not me.'

'Yes, but I'm not on the inside – yet.'

'So you say. Then why ask me about this kid? The kid hanging around.'

'That doesn't put me on the inside. It may be a wrong tip, anyway.'

'Tell me, and see if I can help.'

'At this stage I couldn't if I wanted to. I'm handicapped by my official position.'

Dixie roared with laughter. 'You're *handicapped!*' he jeered when he could speak. 'Hell, your official position is all you've got. If you were working on a commission basis you'd starve.'

Martineau had to grin. Dixie was amusing sometimes. 'Let's keep the chatter on the main subject, shall we?' he suggested.

'Sure, sure. Let's see. You came here hoping I'd tell you who did a shooting job I know nothing about. So I can't tell you.'

'So?'

'Well, I shall certainly make inquiries. I want to find that cowboy as much as you do. I can't afford to have my friends seen off in bundles of two.'

'That's something I wanted to talk to you about. If you happen to find this fellow, I want him. In one piece, not carved up.'

'You're prehistoric. We're not racecourse boys these days.'

'Come off it. You're not talking to the *Daily News*. I know every one of those roughriders of yours.'

'They don't use guns,' said Dixie softly.

'Not until now, they don't. I'm warning you, Dixie. I think you know all about this job, already. I think you'll start looking for one certain person as soon as I've turned my back. You can please yourself about that, but if there's any unlicensed butchery, I'll make you cry.'

The boss mobster did not raise his voice. 'Inspector,' he said, 'neither you, nor the sergeant there, nor your whole bloody police force can make Dixie Costello cry.'

Martineau grinned. 'Just one bobby will do it, Dixie,' he said. 'Just the single one.'

2

DETECTIVE SUPERINTENDENT CLAY always started work at nine o'clock in the morning. Usually he went home at six, but sometimes at eight and sometimes at eleven, and occasionally at two in the morning. Nevertheless, he was always on duty at nine.

Martineau, who had climbed into bed at four o'clock on the morning of the Burleigh Street killings, was also on duty at nine o'clock the same morning. He gave Clay five minutes to settle his thick, solid body at his desk, then he went to see him.

Clay had a thick sheaf of crime reports in front of him, and he had already looked at the headings. 'Ah, Martineau,' he said. 'Come in and sit down. You've got a job, I believe. There's no report here.'

'I was on it till three-thirty, sir.'

Clay nodded. 'All right. Tell me about it.'

Martineau told him. 'No surgeon's report yet,' he concluded.

Again Clay nodded. 'We know they're dead, and that will do to be going on with,' he said. 'That's two villains who'll give us no more bother.'

'They might give us a lot, before we've cleared the job.'

'Troublesome alive and troublesome dead, eh? I don't know. Costello might get things moving for us. He has his reputation to think of. Nobody is supposed to touch any of his mob.'

'I'm tolerably certain that he knows more than we do. He didn't really try to get any information from me, he only tried to find out how much I knew.'

'You and Costello trying to pump each other is my

definition of wasted energy. You did well to make him show anything at all. We can take a small chance on the theory that Kaplan and Ray were operating on his behalf and not on their own. We can also assume that there was some big stuff involved. The only big stuff which has disturbed my nights recently is the twenty thousand pounds from the Northern Counties Bank job. Inspector Pearson isn't making much headway with that, though he's trying hard enough in all conscience.'

'Twenty thousand in new one-pound notes, not yet issued and all the numbers known? Would Costello touch anything like that?'

'You know him as well as I do. Ask yourself, don't ask me.'

'He might have a channel for new money. So long as he didn't have to touch anything with his own dirty fingers, he might have a bash at it.'

'I can't see Costello behind the bank job. If he stole so much money it wouldn't be carried about the streets by two of his men. I see Costello as the man who tries to rob the bank robbers. That would be right up his street.'

'So, as Mr. Anonymous tells us, Kaplan and Ray were trying to do a hold-up job when they were shot.'

'That's the way it looks to me.'

Martineau pondered aloud. 'The anonymous yarn about a fibre suitcase has given us all the idea that something of value was being carried by somebody. Also it provides a feasible motive or reason for the crime. We might be thinking exactly as someone intends us to think. The brown fibre suitcase might be entirely imaginary.'

There was a knock on the door. 'Come in,' Clay called.

The door was opened by one of the gaolers on duty. 'There's something here addressed to you, sir,' he said. 'I found it behind the main gate in the yard.'

He was holding a battered suitcase, obviously made of cardboard or fibre, brown in colour. There was a tie-on label attached to the handle. He brought the case to the desk, and both the C.I.D. men read the writing on the label: 'For Det. Supt. Clay. Evidence re the Burleigh Street shootings'.

'Well, that beats cockfighting,' said Clay. 'When did you find this?'

'Just a minute ago, sir. It can't have been there long. Somebody would have seen it.'

'I knew this was going to be a comic job,' Martineau muttered, and the remark went unheeded.

Clay was frowning in thought. 'We'll put up a notice, asking if any of the men have seen a suspicious-looking person near the gate,' he said. 'That's all we can do in the way of immediate inquiry.' He nodded to the gaoler. 'Open that thing and see what's inside.'

The gaoler slipped the two catches on the case and raised the lid. 'Empty, sir,' he said. He closed the case, and at a further nod from the C.I.D. chief he withdrew.

'Somebody knows who you are and what your job is, at any rate,' Martineau observed.

'Any ordinary local tea-leaf knows that.'

'You can hardly call this client ordinary, or the job either. First we have an anonymous informer. Then we have, apparently, a murderer who supplies us with evidence. It's barmy.'

'He's not going to be traced through his writing,' said Clay, looking at the label. 'Block letters and a ball-point pen.'

'It might be a good idea if we looked at the actual report of the man who received the tip-off from Anonymous. The words "justifiable homicide" were used, I believe. That doesn't sound like the language of the man in the street.'

Clay spoke on the internal line, and the report, which would later be the second item in the Burleigh Street file, was brought to him. He and Martineau perused it. There was no more direct information in it than had been given to Martineau on the telephone, but there were verbatim phrases which interested him. 'Look at this,' he said. ' "I wish to report a shooting affray in Burleigh Road!" '

'I'm with you,' said Clay. 'See here, when he was asked for his name. "I prefer to remain anonymous." '

'And here, when our man tried to detain him in argument. "You've got your information and your suspect, you don't need my evidence yet. You're not going to clear the job in five minutes." '

'It's proper police jargon. He was excited or nervous, and he gave himself away. He doesn't talk like a crook, he talks like a policeman.'

'A policeman or an ex.'

'Either way, we've got a chance of finding him. I'll make every man in the force prove where he was at the time of the shooting. Anybody who can't satisfy me is in for a warm session.'

'This man talks as if he might come forward when we really need him. A serving officer wouldn't do that, after he'd refused to give his name in the first place. He'd know he'd get the sack for that.'

'How about a policeman on pension?'

'Possible. But bobbies on pension don't make a practice of acting the goat. A pension can be forfeited. My fancy is an ex-policeman with no pension to lose. He's drawn his superannuation contributions and he's clear. Neither the police authorities nor the Home Office can touch him until he actually breaks the law.'

'Why *is* he behaving in this damn silly way? A man who has been a policeman! It's downright disloyal.'

'Happen we'll understand his motives when we've talked to him. First, let's find him.'

'All right. You go to work on the ex-policemen. I'll attend to serving men and pensioners. Also, I'll set Sergeant Bird to work on this suitcase, and then it can go to the laboratory. We'll see if it can tell us any sort of a story.'

'Last night it would have told us the story. I wonder who has the contents. That seems like the biggest puzzle of the whole business. A man carrying something valuable in a suitcase. He shoots two men to keep the stuff. So it doesn't look as if anybody can have taken it away from him. Then the case arrives here. If it *is* the case. The thing doesn't make sense. And furthermore there's been nothing yet to compel me to believe anything except the bare fact that Bert Kaplan and Joe Ray have shuffled off this mortal coil.'

Clay grinned. 'You know what to do,' he said. 'Get busy.'

.   .   .   .   .

After a busy day, which would probably be followed by a busy evening, Martineau and Devery went across the street for a glass of beer. On the way Devery bought a local newspaper, the *Evening Guardian*. He tucked the paper unopened under his arm, and it was still unopened when he took the first drink of his second beer. He expected that it would contain news of murder coupled with his own name and Martineau's, but he was in no hurry to read.

He was soon made anxious to read. A man farther along the bar spoke to the barmaid. 'I say, Carrie. Somebody in Granchester has found ten thousand quid in the street.'

The two policemen turned quickly. The man was holding an *Evening Guardian*. Martineau started towards him, then stopped when Devery began to open his own paper. Both men peered at the double page of small advertisements. 'There it is,' said Martineau, putting a large forefinger on the 'Found' column.

It had been said of the *Evening Guardian* that it would announce the end of the world with quarter-inch headlines. On this occasion the tradition was maintained. Calmly, tongue in cheek, knowing that he had a sensation which would make the newspapers of the land shout their questions in large type, the editor had taken the opportunity to chalk up one more anecdote about his own and his paper's imperturbability. Upon his instructions the advertisement had been given no more prominence than the announcements concerning gloves, umbrellas, dogs, kittens and spare wheels which surrounded it. The item was brief: 'FOUND in a Granchester street early this morning, ten thousand (10,000) pounds in notes. Claimant will be required to name form of parcel, denominations of notes, place, time

14

and circumstances in which they were lost. Apply Box G96, or any police station.'

'Any police station,' Martineau breathed. 'The nerve of the man!'

'It's a dodge,' said Devery. 'The man who has the money wants to give the impression that the police have it. He'll feel safer that way.'

'He'll feel safer still in clink.'

'On what charge? If he wanted to steal the money, all he had to do was sit tight and say nothing.'

'Where's a phone?' Martineau snarled. 'I see Butler's fine Italian hand in this. I want to know if he's still on the premises.'

By a telephone call to the *Evening Guardian* offices he learned that Mr. Butler, the News Editor, was still there. 'Tell him not to go home,' Martineau rasped. 'I'll be with him in five minutes.'

Butler was in his office. Grinning, he rose to meet a fuming Martineau and a serious Devery. He shook hands cordially. 'Sit down, gentlemen,' he said. 'We knew there would be a visit from the police, and I volunteered to stay and bear the brunt of it.'

'Why didn't you let us know as soon as the advert came in?' Martineau demanded.

'I can think of no reason in favour of that, and one reason against it.'

'Name it.'

'We didn't want to give the impression that we expected the police to go running around trying to trace the perpetrator of a hoax.'

'That's a nice line of chatter. I'll grant you it could be a hoax. But it isn't likely in view of recent events.'

'Do you mean that this money – assuming that it *has* been found – has some connexion with the murders in Burleigh Street last night?'

Suddenly Martineau became cautious. 'I can't say anything about that, yet. But ten thousand pounds, man! You ought to have tipped us off.'

'Did we have a legal obligation?'

'No, I don't think so. But there is supposed to be a bit of give and take between the police and the Press, isn't there?'

'What good would it have done you, to know?'

'That's something you never know, in police work. You can't assess the value of information you didn't get.'

Butler became candid. 'We talked it over and didn't see how it would help, but I'll admit we all wanted to keep it to ourselves till we'd made our scoop.'

'Is it a scoop? Is there any chance that it will pass unnoticed by other newspapers?'

'Good Lord, no! All our reporters are busy making lineage money, passing the news on to morning papers up and down the country. They'll all have it tomorrow.'

Martineau nodded gloomily. 'I can see what will happen.'

'But of course. You've got two first-class mysteries. The ace sensation-mongers of all the national newspapers will be here at the double, trying to link them together. You'll find reporters floating in your morning tea.'

'Very well. We'll do what we can before they arrive. What time did the advert come in?'

'The mid-morning post. The envelope was postmarked Granchester, seven-thirty. A one-pound note was enclosed with the letter, and instructions to give the change to a deserving charity. Here they are; envelope, letter, and banknote.'

'One crafty client,' the chief inspector muttered, taking the pieces of paper gingerly. 'Signed "A. Walker". Block letters again. Cheap paper and envelope. Can I borrow these?'

'Certainly.'

'There'll be claims and begging letters from every fraud and scrounger in the north of England. One of those claims might be important. I'll want to see the letters as soon as they come in.'

'Over the dead bodies of the entire staff of the *Evening Guardian*. Those letters will be the property of the advertiser.'

16

'We'll see about that. In any case I would like to have two men in the office, out of sight. They can be given the griff as soon as anybody calls for the letters.'

'I think we can agree to that. But it's my opinion that nobody will call. I think we'll receive a letter of instructions and a large, stamped-addressed envelope.'

'That's all the same. Our men can be shown the envelope.'

'That's fair enough, so long as they don't try to get possession of it. Anything else?'

'No,' said Martineau, in a better mood now. 'You can go home and have your tea, while I slave away through the night, making some more news for you to misinterpret.'

'You don't make news, you suppress it,' was the good-humoured retort.

.   .   .   .   .

Martineau and Devery walked the short distance back to Headquarters. Almost every group of people they passed seemed to be discussing the *Evening Guardian*. There was no doubt that the coincidence of a double murder in mysterious circumstances and a matter of ten thousand pounds without an owner would excite great public interest.

'Well, how do you like it now?' Martineau asked.

'I think we should believe Mr. Anonymous,' Devery replied without hesitation. 'He gives us something to work on. Ten thousand pounds in a fibre suitcase, being carried through the streets. It wouldn't be intended to carry it far. A few hundred yards from some place to a car.'

'Yes. Now the fellows working the Burleigh Street district have something definite to look for, and maybe they've already found it without knowing it. At about twelve o'clock last night there was a meeting in some place around there. If we can find the place, we might be a bit nearer to knowing something. There might have been a meeting for the purpose of splitting the Northern Counties Bank plunder. Either Kaplan and Ray, or Leatherjacket got half the takings. Leatherjacket got it eventually, we know that.'

'And then went crackers? Sent the suitcase to the police and advertised the money in the Press?'

'You've got me there. But remember that both the suitcase and the advert might be fakes. They might be part of some deep dodge we haven't fathomed yet. They might have been arranged by somebody who's trying to shake down Leatherjacket. Let's find that meeting place, and see if it gets us any nearer to the truth.'

3

On the day following the shooting of Kaplan and Ray, the area around the scene of the crime had been thoroughly covered by a team of detectives. But their inquiries had had the object of finding witnesses, finding persons who had seen or heard anything or anybody to make them suspicious, and seeking evidence generally. On the morning following that day of toil Martineau called the men before him. There were six detectives, of whom one was a sergeant.

'Now,' said the chief inspector. 'You had a good look round yesterday. Did you all have a separate area to work?'

'All except me,' said the sergeant. 'I went from man to man, seeing how they were getting on.'

'Very good. Today each man will take the area he had yesterday, and the sergeant will sit in the office with the Post Office Directory under his nose. The object is to find a place where there was a divvy-up of plunder a little while before the Burleigh Street job. The place could have been the office of some fly-by-night concern which hasn't been in existence a month. Do you get the idea? The sergeant will fix you up with times to ring in. Any place which doesn't seem solid, any place you aren't quite certain about, you'll put them on your list. You'll ring them in. The sergeant will look them up in the directory. Sergeant, by three o'clock this afternoon I expect you to give me a list of all the little businesses around Burleigh Street which are *not* in the directory. Meaning that they haven't been there long enough to get in the directory. Is everything understood?'

Apparently everything was. Martineau sent the men about their business and went to attend to his own, which was to report to Chief Superintendent Clay all that was afoot. The surgeon's report was discussed, and some mis-shapen bullets were examined. There was some hope expressed that the two experienced detectives now lying in wait at the *Evening Guardian* office might have some luck. Then Clay had to go upstairs for his daily conference with the Chief Constable.

Clay was still upstairs and Martineau was back in his own office when the forlorn hope was realized in a curious way. One of the two policemen at the newspaper office telephoned the chief inspector and admitted that he was in doubt as to how he should act. He explained: 'We've collared a fellow here, asking for the replies to the G96 advert, and he wants to know whether or not he's under arrest.'

'Of course—' Martineau began, and then he stopped. After a thoughtful pause he said: 'Can't you get him to come here with you, without actually arresting him?'

'No. He's wise to that. He seems to know the game.'

'Ah. An ex-policeman?'

'Definitely not, sir. I think he's a lawyer. What's more, I think he's being awkward for the sake of it. He's sort of good-humoured about it, but he's threatening to walk away from us. He says we can't hold him here.'

'Don't let him walk away from you!' Martineau warned.

'Very good, sir. So what do we do?'

'Bring him in, but don't use force unless you have to. If he wants an explanation, tell him you're acting on my direct order. Bring him here to me.'

'Right you are, sir,' said the detective, much relieved.

And ten minutes later he and his colleague ushered a short, sturdy young man into Martineau's office. His ruddy, pleasant face advertised cleanliness and good living. He was not one of your dry-as-dust lawyers; he wore tweeds and a sporty waistcoat. An outdoor man.

'On what pretext have I been brought here?' he demanded, grimly equable.

'Reasonable suspicion,' replied Martineau, equally calm.

'Of what?'

'Reasonable suspicion that a crime has been committed.'

20

'There are no grounds for such a suspicion. Everything
has been done quite legally. Your men had no right to bring
me here.'

'So what are you going to do about it?' came the blunt
challenge.

That made the young man pause. 'I may sue,' he said. 'I
have been subjected to public ignominy.'

'I publicly apologise, here and now,' said Martineau, not
at all apologetic.

'That's only a form of words.'

'It's all it is intended to be. This whole thing is technical.
Sue if you like. You're not likely to win. If you do, you'll get
a farthing damages and a lot more public ignominy. Now
then, why don't you behave reasonably and tell me why
you're trying to annoy the police?'

The young man grinned suddenly. 'I don't like bobbies,'
he said. 'I got done for speeding a month ago. The man was
a confounded liar.'

Martineau looked bored. 'The policeman always is, in a
speeding case,' he said. 'What sort of a car have you
got?'

'I don't see what that has got to do with it.'

'He's got a three-point-four Jag,' said one of the detectives. 'He brought us here in it.'

'One of the fastest cars on the road. Think of all the times
you've speeded and got away with it. Now, what is your
name?'

'Roger Slade.'

'Of Hunter, Charteris and Slade, by any chance?'

'Yes. How did you guess that?'

'My men thought you were a lawyer, and I happen to
know your father. Does he know about this business?'

'No, he's out of town.'

'Well, I'm not supposing that you're the man who found
ten thousand pounds. Are you acting for him?'

'Yes, and I'm not going to tell you a damn thing about
him. You can't make me talk about my client.'

'That's all right. We'll find him without your help. But I

think you should tell us one or two things. For instance, is the money safe?'

'As safe as money could be. Take my word for it.'

'Very well. Is it in notes?'

'Yes.'

'One-pound notes?'

'Yes, all of it.'

'New or old?'

'Used notes. If it had been new money I would immediately have connected it with the robbery at the Northern Counties Bank.'

'And don't you so connect it?'

'Of course not.'

'Well, well,' said Martineau. 'You're a very young solicitor, aren't you? Why did you call for the G96 replies so early? Curiosity?'

The pleasant, slightly mischievous grin reappeared. 'I wanted to see what would happen,' Slade admitted. 'That's why I went to the *Evening Guardian* myself instead of sending an articled clerk. I thought the bobbies would be on the job, and I wanted to have a bit of fun with them.'

'You *are* a young solicitor. Is that why you took the business on, for laughs?'

'I suppose so. I guessed the police would be in a lather about it. My word, have you seen the papers this morning?'

'I've seen the headlines. Didn't you advise your client to hand over the money to the police?'

'He had already put it in a safe deposit, and he left the key with me. I got my insurance man on the job. We insured it, on the condition that the money could not be taken from the safe deposit except in the presence of all three of us.'

'That seems to be good enough. But you know that it is customary to hand over found property to the police.'

'It's so customary that a lot of people think it's a legal obligation. But *you* should know the law of the matter.'

'I may not know it all. You tell me.'

'The finder of property which is not Treasure Trove has

a legal right to it over everyone except the actual owner. Until the owner shows up, the property belongs to the finder. But the finder has a legal obligation to make an effort to find the owner, otherwise he is guilty of Stealing by Finding. An announcement in a local newspaper is usually considered to be an adequate effort. In the case of a sum of money like ten thousand pounds, one insertion of the announcement is sufficient. Every newspaper in the land is following it up.'

'Very succinct. And assuming that there is no valid claim to the money, how many days will elapse before it becomes the absolute property of the finder?'

'I thought you would trot that one out. We'll cross that bridge when we come to it. The Granchester police usually hand over property to the finder if it hasn't been claimed after three months, don't they? Neither myself nor my client believe that they would stick to that routine in the case of ten thousand pounds. It's too much money.'

'What do you suppose will happen, then?'

'Very likely there'll be a valid claim. That depends on the police to some extent. If there is no claim, my client hopes to have the use of the money after a time. He will be satisfied with that. He doesn't even hope that he will ever become the absolute owner, though it *is* possible that he and his heirs will have the use of the money until the lapse of time cancels all probability of a successful claim to it.'

'Why do you say that a valid claim depends on the police?'

'A slip of the tongue.'

'Don't you think that as a good citizen you ought to tell me more?'

Once more the infectious grin appeared. 'How dull to be a good citizen. I'm a criminal, a menace who drives at thirty-six miles an hour in York Road in a car with disc brakes.'

'It's a built-up area. I still think you should tell me more.'

'No. My client should tell you more. I can't.'

'He knows something, then?'

'No comment.'

'Can you get him to give you the full story for us?'

'I'll try.'

'I don't see why he doesn't come forward like an honest man. He's got the money wrapped up safe enough.'

'Perhaps he's bashful.'

'We'll find him, you know. He's an ex-policeman, isn't he?'

'Well, well,' Slade breathed. And then he said: 'The usual no comment.'

Martineau suddenly beamed. He was all affability – and sarcasm. 'Thank you, Mr. Slade,' he said. 'You are at liberty to go, and we do all apologise most sincerely for any trouble we may have caused you. Please do call upon us if we can help you in any way.'

'Coo, coppers,' said Mr. Slade. 'Cheerio.'

'Cheerio,' said Martineau. And when the newly-fledged solicitor had departed he turned to Devery. 'A nice young man. I like him,' he said. 'There's not much use trying to tie a tail to him with a car like he's got. Stake out his house and his office with two men each. Any ex-policeman who calls on him had better be brought here for interrogation.'

.   .   .   .   .

Before the deadline of three o'clock that afternoon, Detective Sergeant Patterson brought to Martineau a list of business concerns in the Burleigh Street district.

'None of these are in the Post Office Directory, sir,' he said. 'Some of them seem to be middling dodgy, according to reports.'

The chief inspector took the three-page list of names and addresses, and said with satisfaction: 'Plenty to go at there. Let's see if there is anything which will give us a what-you-call-it, a clue.'

He perused the list, and when he had read to the end he turned back to the second page. 'Acropolis Trading Company,' he said. 'Now then, you Greek scholars, what does "Acropolis" mean?'

24

'I think it will mean "top of the town" or something like that,' Devery ventured. 'I believe the Acropolis itself is on a hill above Athens.'

'The top, anyway,' said Martineau. 'I'll have to get a search warrant.' And as the two sergeants looked at each other with raised eyebrows he went on: 'You'll need the keys, Devery. Sergeant Patterson, I shall want you and four men. We'll need two cars.'

When the warrant had been secured, Martineau walked out of the police building and found that all was in readiness. He got into the front seat of a C.I.D. car beside Devery, nodded to the detective in the rear seat, and said in high good humour: 'Forward. Advance upon the Acropolis.'

Devery set the car smoothly in motion. 'I've been trying to work it out,' he said. 'Why did you choose that particular one?'

'Because I'm a man with some service in, my young cockerel. The older you get, the more you know. Did you ever hear of the Summit Supplies job?'

'No sir. I can't say I ever did.'

'Did you ever hear of it, Cassidy?'

'No sorr. It must have been before me toime,' said Cassidy, who only spoke with the brogue when he wanted to. He used it with intent, often in subtle mockery of the English: the simple Irishman who was not simple at all.

'Summit Supplies yielded us the finest collection of stolen property it has ever been my pleasure to see. But it ran for about five years before we got wind of it, and somebody had made plenty. A fellow called Goosey Bright got five years for that. If he had any partners, he forgot to mention the fact. He took it for the lot. He came out of the nick about seven years ago, and as far as I know he's lived in Birmingham since. Except that I got a whisper a week or two ago saying he was back home in Granchester again.'

'Is that the only line you've got, sir?' Devery asked in surprise. 'Summit and Acropolis twelve years apart seems a bit slender.'

'Ah, but I took the trouble to read Goosey's biography.

25

There'd been Peak Imports and Paramount Products and Acme Trading. Goosey seems to fancy the top as a target, bless his little heart, and I don't think he dreams that any copper has tumbled to his little fad.'

'In that case there might be something in it, sir.'

'We hope so,' said Martineau smugly.

The Acropolis Trading Company had its premises in a shabby block of offices which was sandwiched between two small warehouses. It was a hundred yards from Burleigh Street, and two hundred yards from the spot where Kaplan and Ray had kept their appointment with death. Sergeant Patterson attended to the matter of guarding front and rear entrances, and Martineau, Devery and Cassidy climbed the narrow, linoleum-covered stairs to the top floor. A door which had not had a coat of paint in years bore the newly-painted designation of the company. The chief inspector tried the door. It was locked. His peremptory knock was not answered.

He nodded to Devery. 'Get weaving.'

The sergeant stooped to examine the lock. He selected a key from the big ring of master keys which he carried. He tried the key in the lock, and kept on trying keys until he found one which would move the wards of the lock. The business of opening the door took three minutes, but no damage was done.

'This may really be Inspector Pearson's job,' said Martineau as he led the way into the premises. 'But we won't bother him until we've found something.'

The three men looked around the place. The Acropolis Trading Company had two small rooms, comprising an outer and an inner office. The outer office was a waiting room with a worn carpet, some chairs, a round table and a baggy old sofa. The door of the inner office had been inscribed with the word 'Private' some years ago. It was not locked.

The inner office had two desks, one of which supported a typewriter which looked as if it could be made to rattle convincingly. There was a wastepaper basket which was

26

quite empty, a worn rug between the desks, some filing cabinets, an ancient safe, two desk chairs, and two arm-chairs which belonged to the same family as the sofa in the other room. 'Ten pounds the lot,' said Cassidy.

The filing cabinets were not locked, and they contained nothing but venerable layers of Granchester grime. The safe was unlocked and likewise empty. All but one of the desk drawers were locked. The open one contained an assortment of used type erasers, broken pencils, odd paper clips and other office debris, and it was possible that these had been left by the tenant who preceded the Acropolis man. It also contained the keys to all the other drawers, which were opened and found to be empty.

'Goosey or no Goosey,' said Martineau. 'Somebody has skipped and left the place clean.'

He lifted up the rug and looked at the underside. Devery tilted up one armchair and Cassidy the other. They searched the armchairs. They began a systematic search of the room. Martineau looked thoughtfully at the bigger of the two desks. 'Heave me that up,' he said. 'Let me see under-neath.'

There was nothing but dust under the desk. In disgust, Martineau gave the wastepaper basket a hearty kick. It flew across the room and bounced off the wall. Devery was watching, and his keen eyes saw a tiny white pellet on the floor. It had not been there before Martineau kicked the basket. He pounced upon it. It was a pellet of paper so small that it had slipped into an interstice of the wicker-work and had been concealed there. He unfolded it. 'Look at this,' he said.

Carelessly written on the fragment of torn paper was a cipher and part of a cipher at the irregular edge, and the number S95K665999. 'The second one looks like the number of a banknote,' he said.

Martineau peered. 'The first one might be part of a banknote number, too,' he said. 'A number ending in two noughts.'

He thought for a moment. 'The nearest number ending

27

in two noughts is nine hundred,' he said. 'Subtract and you get ninety-nine. That's a comic number.'

'Not at all,' said Devery, his tense excitement suddenly changing to elation. 'The Northern Counties twenty thousand was in bundles of five hundred, each bundle tied with white tape. According to the description every bundle had a numbered ticket pushed under the tape.'

'I see what you mean. This ticket could have been S95K665500 and S95K665999, the lowest and highest numbers of a bundle of five hundred. We're on the track of the bank's money.'

'And we know the story.'

'Yes, it's just as we thought. There was a deal, new money for old. Two nice new notes for one old crumpled bookie's sweetheart. This place is where they traded a hot twenty thousand for a cool ten. And then they tried to steal the ten back, and two of 'em got themselves killed. Serve 'em right.'

'Justifiable homicide, as Mr. Anonymous said?'

'It could be. He witnessed it all right. I wonder if he knows the entire story.'

'We might get to know that when we find him.'

'Yes. But right now we had better get Pearson on the job. I notice there's no phone here. Cassidy, get out to the car and try to contact Inspector Pearson. Tell him that if he'll come here quickly, he might hear something to his advantage.'

'He'll be after Goosey like a – like a fox,' said Devery.

'Yes, if it *was* Goosey who had this place. There might be some fingerprints.'

'You weren't really so sure that this might be Goosey's place, then?'

'No, it was just the long chance,' said Martineau comfortably. 'My neighbour has a black cat which comes and sits on our doorstep, waiting for my wife to give it a bit of breakfast. I accidentally kicked it this morning when I was turning out for work. It made me think I might have a bit of luck today.'

4

DETECTIVE INSPECTOR PEARSON discovered the
fingerprints of Goosey Bright in the Acropolis premises, and
went after him not like a fox, but with the uneasy eagerness
of a terrier. His satisfaction in having a suspect was clouded
by sickening apprehension. The twenty thousand pounds
of bank money had been moved from the Acropolis
premises. Inspector Pearson's fear was that it had been
moved to a place beyond his reach.

The word went out. Almost the entire force was deployed
in the hunt for Goosey. Exits from the town were picketed.
If Goosey and his ill-gotten gains were still in Granchester,
they would not get out. If they were still on the island of
Britain, there was a good chance that they would be found.
If they had left the country . . . Interpol was informed.

But Inspector Pearson had a fluttering in his tight little
beginning of a paunch. He wanted Goosey in Granchester.
He had more faith in Inspector Pearson than in Interpol.

The activity was such that the crack newshounds who now
haunted Headquarters heard the mention of Goosey's name.
It sounded like good copy to them. They clamoured to
know. Who was this man? Was he a murder suspect? Did
he have something to do with the ten thousand pounds
which had been found?

The busy detectives making their inquiries in curt, tight-
mouthed phrases indirectly transmitted the news to the
criminal, semi-criminal and occasionally criminal elements
in the city. Informers, mindful of the reward offered by the
bank for information leading to the recovery of its money,
became so avid in the quest for 'the griff' that some of them
betrayed themselves instead of Goosey. During all this
bustle Martineau sat quietly in his office. He waited for

news of Anonymous, and he also hoped to hear from a certain Pot Eye Walker, an old friend who was in the habit of touching him for small loans. It had been said of Pot Eye that he could see more with his artificial optic than most men could perceive with two good ones, and he had been Martineau's informer for years. Pot Eye was the man who had whispered to the chief inspector that Goosey was back in town, and he was the man most likely to be able to put a finger on Goosey, but Martineau was in some doubt about his willingness to do so. Two men had been killed already. The reward of one thousand pounds would seem like a fortune to Pot Eye, but he would make no attempt to secure it if he thought that an expensive funeral was the only benefit he would get from it.

The afternoon passed and darkness fell. A fine, mild night it was, a matter for satisfaction which nobody mentioned to Inspector Pearson, who had become so irascible that he was unfit to be in decent company. Like Martineau he waited.

At five minutes to eight the call came, for Martineau. It was Pot Eye speaking from a public call box, which, if it was illuminated, was always a dangerous place for an informer after dark. He was hoarse with fear, and tremulous with anxiety arising from a deep distrust of human nature.

'You're wanting Goosey Bright,' he began.

'That's right,' Martineau answered tersely, pulling forward a note pad and picking up a pencil.

'You reckernize my voice?'

'I do indeed, old rascal.'

'There's some noise outside here, I don't reckernize yours. Say the word as usual.'

'Angel of Mons.'

'That's it, that's it. Has the big reward aught to do with Goosey?'

'It might have.'

'Could I get it?'

'You could.'

'Then get your skates on. Everest Export Company,

Grange Street, next door to the garridge. Goosey is standing behind the door there, watching 'em load a van wi' big cartons.'

'Thanks,' said Martineau, already on his feet.

He ran out into the main C.I.D. office. Devery and Cassidy were there, busy or pretending to be busy with paper work. 'Get Pearson, quick!' the chief inspector snapped to the sergeant, and ran out. Cassidy followed him.

Outside the building there was just one car, and it was the Chief Constable's. The uniformed driver stood beside it. 'I'm afraid I'll have to borrow you for ten minutes, Briggs,' said Martineau.

'The Chief said he'd be only a minute,' the man replied with a shake of the head.

Martineau ran round the car and took the seat behind the wheel. Cassidy climbed in beside him as Devery and Pearson ran from the building. The Chief came striding out at the same time, and they muttered apologies as they passed him.

'Damn and blast,' said Martineau under his breath when he saw the Chief.

'What's all this?' the great man wanted to know.

'A job, sir. Important and terribly urgent. I took the liberty—'

'Get in, get in,' said the Chief to Devery and Pearson. 'And make room for me.'

Grange Street was in the middle of town near one of the main railway stations, and only three minutes drive from Police Headquarters at that time in the evening. Had it been farther away than that, the police would have been too late. A carrier's van was beginning to draw away from the Everest Export Company when the Chief's car arrived. Martineau put the car alongside the van.

'Police! Pull in and pull up!' he bellowed.

The van stopped immediately, and so did the car. The policemen scrambled out. Martineau pointed to a man who dashed out of the Everest doorway and ran along the street. 'Get him,' he said to Devery, who could run faster than he.

31

Then he ran round the van to confront the driver as he alighted.

'What's up?' that person asked nervously.

'What have you got in the van?'

'A mixed load for Hull.'

'What did you take on here?'

'Ten cartons o' chocolates.'

Martineau turned to Pearson. 'I think you'll want those cartons. That was Goosey Bright who just ran away.'

He looked along the street and saw Devery returning, with Goosey walking tamely beside him. They came up. Goosey was still breathing heavily. He was a tall, middle-aged man with a big belly, bottle shoulders, a long neck, little angry eyes and a long nose who did indeed have some of the appearance of a rather peevish gander. If he was downcast, he did not show it. Anger was his emotion.

'We're going to search your place,' Pearson said. 'Do we get a warrant, or will you give us permission?'

'I'll give you nothing,' said Goosey.

Pearson shrugged. 'Ride in the front of the van with him,' he said to Devery. 'I'll ride in the back with the cartons. Cassidy, you stay and keep an eye on this place until I send somebody with a warrant.' He looked at the Chief. 'I think we can go back to Headquarters now, sir.'

'Certainly,' said the Chief, and turned to his own car. He sat in the front with Martineau. 'Has that man stolen the chocolates, or is it less simple than that?' he asked.

'Less simple, sir. We are after the twenty thousand pounds stolen from the Northern Counties Bank.'

'H'm. It was an important and urgent job, as you remarked,' said the Chief.

Goosey's ten cartons were unloaded in the police station yard. They were big, heavy, and firmly wired. Stencilling indicated that they had been bound for Antwerp. The names of shipping agents were clearly inked, and the agents' marks appeared to be genuine. Wire cutters were obtained, and one of the cartons was opened. It was neatly filled with cardboard boxes, each of which contained an ornate box of locally-made chocolates. Pearson made a face when he saw them. 'I hope we find the money,' he said. 'If we don't, we're in trouble.'

He stood in thought, while the others waited. 'I know what we'll do,' he said. 'In the Weights and Measures office there'll be some scales. We'll weigh each one of these chocolate boxes and see if any of them are off the norm.'

The scales were brought and men were set to work unpacking, weighing, and putting aside. A box from the third layer of the fourth carton opened weighed a few ounces more than any which had been weighed so far. With eager fingers Pearson ripped away the transparent wrapping and lifted off the lid. Neatly fitted into the box were two solid wads of new one-pound notes. When they had been taken out of the box it was found that the numbers of the notes in each wad ran consecutively. When one wad was put on top of the other, there was a stack of five hundred notes.

Pearson was exultant. 'That's the first bundle,' he crowed. 'We only want thirty-nine more.'

. . . . .

A policeman less persistent than Martineau would have called the arrest of Goosey Bright a good day's work. Though that was Inspector Pearson's case in the book, it was Martineau who had received the necessary information and acted promptly to prevent the Northern Counties Bank's money from being shipped out of the country. He knew that the Chief Constable, the most important man, would give him credit for the arrest, and he valued the Chief's esteem. Nevertheless, he was dissatisfied with the day's work. His own case, the Kaplan-Ray murder job, seemed to be at a standstill.

So at half-past ten, when he might have been at home having his supper, Martineau was still at Headquarters. He knew that some of his men were still out on the Anonymous inquiry, and as long as they were working, so would he be. At half-past ten Detective Constable Ducklin came to see him. Ducklin was an obsequious subordinate and would someday be an officious superior. Martineau disliked

33

him for his manner, and knew that he was wrong in doing so because an officer with a team of efficient individuals should have no personal preferences. Because of this he always took time for a second thought before he let Ducklin know the rough side of his tongue. There was a general impression in the C.I.D. that he had a special liking for the man.

On this occasion Ducklin's air of studied nonchalance was just about as deceptive as a halo. He had done something which would merit praise. He was confidently stepping forward and up.

'I looked up Cliff Eaglan this evening, sir,' he began.

Martineau nodded, waiting for the whole story. Like a reporter with a news item, Ducklin had told his tale in one sentence to rivet attention, and would follow with the details. So it was Eaglan, who had been one of Martineau's own men. A good man, too. But now a man with a grievance, probably. He had been dismissed from the force.

'I asked Eaglan about his movements at the time of the shooting,' Ducklin went on. 'He might have been at home in bed, but he wouldn't say so. He told me to go to hell. I kept at him for a while, then I left him.'

Martineau waited. There was more to come. He had to hear how painstaking Ducklin had been.

The detective continued: 'I wasn't satisfied, and I wondered how I could get at him. I remembered I had once seen him with Florrie Kitts. Florrie likes bobbies.'

Martineau nodded again. There are girls who like policemen, just as there are girls who like footballers and girls who love sailors.

Said Ducklin: 'She lives in Pitt Street, not too far from Burleigh Street. I thought I'd give her the once over. She was out, and it took me two hours to find her. When I did, she came through all right. I have a statement which says she was with Eaglan the evening before the shooting. Met him in the Northland Hotel. He took her home and kept her out till after twelve. Without avail, so she says.'

'He left her between twelve and half-past, and went towards Burleigh Street?'

'That's right, sir.'

'Very good. You're doing very well. Now go and get him.'

'Without a warrant? He might be in bed.'

'Tell him he can ride here in a police car of his own free will, or sit on the edge of his bed till I arrive with a warrant and make him walk all the way. If he values his night's rest, he'll come.'

'Verygoodsir!' Ducklin turned, and was gone. A man with a mission.

Martineau sat and thought about Cliff Eaglan before he resumed the paper work which he detested. Not only had Eaglan been a policeman, he had been a member of the Criminal Investigation Department. Because of his knowledge of police work, he was more to be blamed than an ordinary civilian for failing to come forward with a full account of what he had seen in Burleigh Street on the night of the Kaplan-Ray murders. His report of the crime, with the description of the suspect, had been made when it was too late for the police to get busy and intercept the suspect before he reached home. If the report had been made immediately after the shooting, the police might well have picked up the suspect because they would have cordoned that part of the city and would have accosted every man who was on the streets at that time of night. Eaglan must have been well aware of the effect of his delay. It almost looked as if he wanted the murderer to escape. And why not? There might be ten thousand very good reasons why Eaglan wanted the murderer to remain at liberty.

And yet, Martineau reflected, Eaglan *had* reported the murders. Apparently his conscience had troubled him enough to make him at least take half measures.

Ducklin returned to Headquarters shortly after eleven o'clock, and he had Eaglan with him.

'Ex-constable Eaglan, sir,' he said in his unfortunate manner, which immediately elicited a suitable reply. '*Mister* Eaglan to you!' snapped the man who had been an efficient and esteemed police officer only a few months ago.

Martineau thought that Ducklin had been slightly

tactless, but as usual he had no rebuke for the man. 'Sit down, Eaglan,' he said. 'I hope you weren't in bed.'

'No. You'd have had to come for me if I had been. I'd be interested in knowing what you'd have had on the warrant.'

'I hadn't got around to thinking about that,' was the easy reply. 'And of course I don't need to think about it now, since you've come of your own free will.'

'The same old Martineau! What do you want?'

'The full story of what happened in Burleigh Street on Tuesday night, or Wednesday morning to be more exact.'

'Why ask me?'

'We have established you were around there at the time.'

'Can you prove it?'

'We don't need to. Now that we know, there's no point in your denying it, is there?'

Eaglan sat back in his chair and thought about that. Martineau studied him, recalling the incident which had resulted in his dismissal from the force. That incident had been a revelation of instability in a good-looking youngster who had seemed to be big enough both physically and mentally for the job he had held. It had shown a quality curiously disparate from the caution and foresight now being shown in a matter of money.

'You must have had a bit of luck,' Eaglan said with a rueful grin. 'Did Florrie come to you herself?'

'No, we found her.'

'Congratulations. You're right, of course. There's no sense in denying it now. I'm having to talk sooner than I expected, that's all.'

'I'm surprised you didn't come forward right away, a man who used to be a policeman.'

'Out of loyalty, you mean? What I owe to the force? I got sacked, don't you remember?'

'I remember more than you do, seemingly. You broke Sergeant Anstey's nose because you thought he was victimizing you. The inquiry proved quite clearly that he wasn't victimizing you at all, but merely doing what he was compelled to do by the exigencies of the service. And what was it all about? Just a few late turns you thought you shouldn't have had. You could have been sent to prison for that assault, but you weren't even taken to court. You were sacked, but you got your superannuation money back. You have no grudge against the police, boy. You were treated fairly and leniently.'

'I suppose I was,' Eaglan admitted reluctantly. 'I've thought so since. But I could have been allowed to resign.'

'You could have had something out of the poor box, too. And a farewell party. Be honest with yourself, lad. Look, I'll send out for some coffee, and then you can tell me all about this Burleigh Street do.'

5

WITH the coffee came a shorthand writer, who settled himself at a table in the corner. 'Now,' said Martineau. 'We'll skip Florrie and put you in the vicinity of Burleigh Street. What time was it and where were you exactly when the trouble started?'

'It was a couple of minutes short of half past twelve. I had just looked at my watch to see how late I was. I was cutting through the alley into Burleigh Street. Duff's Court, I believe it's called. When I was about forty yards from Burleigh Street I heard somebody call: "Just a minute, kid," and it startled me. I stopped, and as I did so I realized that it wasn't anybody who was talking to me; it was somebody out in the main street. I set off again and I could hear nothing, then I saw a fellow run past the end of the alley carrying a suitcase. He may have been wearing crêpe-soled shoes, because I didn't hear a thing. Then two more fellows ran past, as if they were chasing him. I couldn't hear them, either.'

Martineau nodded. 'They *were* wearing crêpe soles.'

'Yes. Well, I trotted to the end of the alley to see what was up. I saw the three of them still running, but the lad with the suitcase had lost ground. I kept going with the intention of joining in, because I wasn't going to stand still and see somebody robbed. As I ran I noticed that the bloke with the suitcase was wearing a leather jacket, short like a golf jacket. I also saw that he was going to get caught: the suitcase was hampering him too much. He must have realized it himself, because he stopped and turned round. I didn't see the gun at first, but I saw and heard two shots, and Robber Number One went down on his face. Number Two kept going, but Leatherjacket managed to hit him in three more shots, because he fell forward too. But he was a game 'un, and he grabbed for the suitcase as he fell. He was lying sprawling, reaching forward, with either one or both hands on the handle of the suitcase. Leatherjacket belted him on the head a few times with the pistol, but he hung on. Then I'm almost certain Leatherjacket put the gun to this man's head and tried to finish him that way. It looked like that, but there was no shot. Anyway, I was coming steaming up. I'll admit I'd forgotten that I was no longer a copper. Leatherjacket saw me, and he actually tried to shoot *me*. At least he pointed the gun at me, but it didn't go off. He made one last effort and got the suitcase away from Number Two, because Number Two was dead, I suppose. He made off with it, but now he lost ground to me. He turned and tried another shot, but the gun wouldn't work. Either he'd jammed it by banging Number Two's head with it, or else he had no more ammo. So he dropped the suitcase when I nearly had my hands on him, and I fell over it. By the time I got up he was fifty yards away, showing me that he could run all right when he had nothing to carry. I went after him but he ducked down a side street where there are a lot of backyards. I thought he might be hiding there putting his gun to rights, and I also remembered that it wasn't my job to get shot chasing a murderer. So I went back to the suitcase.'

'Had you already guessed that the suitcase would contain something valuable?'

'I hadn't had time. I just went back to it and picked it up. Then I got curious and opened it. I saw that it was full of pound notes, used ones, and I shut it again. I carried it back to where the two dead men were lying, and made sure that they *were* dead. There was no point in calling an ambulance. When men are as dead as Bert Kaplan and Joe Ray were at that moment, I don't need a doctor to tell me.'

'You recognized them, then?'

'Yes, and I knew they were two of Dixie Costello's mob. That made me think a bit. I thought about it while I was walking away with the suitcase. It occurred to me that there might be a thin chance of inheriting the money in the case.

The man who'd had it had killed two men. If he was the owner of the money, he couldn't come forward and claim it without admitting the killings. If the police never arrested him, he might never make his claim.'

'But you could still have handed over the money to the police.'

'I didn't know how they would look at the matter, did I? Possession is nine points of the law. In the circumstances that I got the money, the police might have said that I found it before it was lost.'

'The man abandoned the money, he didn't lose it.'

Eaglan grinned again. 'There you are, you see. I did right to stick to the money. While I have it, the police at least have no claim to it.'

'How about the police wanting to examine the money for fingerprints?'

'On those soiled notes they'd find about a million, I expect.'

It was Martineau's turn to grin. 'All right,' he said. 'Go on with your tale.'

'Well, I walked home, and when I got into my room I had another look at the money. It was in bundles of fifty, and there were two hundred of them. I could have kept the lot and said nothing, but I wouldn't be a thief even for ten thousand quid. And besides, there was one person who knew I'd got it. I shut the case and shoved it under my bed, and went out to report the shooting from a phone box.'

'I presume that your description of the man with the gun is accurate.'

'It was the best I could give.'

'Could you identify him?'

'Yes, I think I could.'

'Had you ever seen him before?'

'No. He was a stranger to me. I suppose you'll want me to look in the picture book.'

'I'd be glad if you would. What was your reason in still keeping away from the police, after you had got the money snug in a safe deposit?'

'Well, who is there in this town big enough to finance a two-for-one deal of that size?'

'You worked that out, did you?'

'Sure. With two of Costello's mob lying dead in the road, it was easy. He gave ten thousand for that twenty thousand of bank money, then arranged to take his own ten thousand back. I don't want him to get wise to me. There's no telling what he might do.'

'He'd be moderately frantic. He's lost the lot.'

Eaglan stared. 'What?'

'We collared a man called Goosey Bright this evening, with all the bank's money.'

'Does he admit that Dixie financed the job?'

'He admits nothing. But we're fairly certain that he couldn't have financed it himself.'

Eaglan was disconsolate. 'There goes my chance of ever being able to use that money,' he said. 'Costello will never let me. He'll harass me in every possible way, trying to get me to hand it over to him. He won't stand a loss of ten thousand.'

'What about Leatherjacket and his associates? They might harass you a bit, too. If they find out who you are.'

'I think they've found out already. Or at least somebody has. It didn't take them long, either.'

'How do you know that?'

'I work for old Isaacson in Newport Street. The radio shop. He's thinking of retiring, and I was sort of hoping I might use some of that ten thousand to take over the business. It could be made into a gold mine. Well, I was out with the van on Wednesday afternoon, passing near my lodgings, and I called to pick up a text-book to take back to the library. I'm studying the job, you see. I went up to my room and found a girl there, lying on the floor on the other side of the bed. The window was wide open, and it looked as if she had climbed in that way. She was wearing a sweater and slacks, and flat-heeled shoes. The palms of her hands were black, as if she had come up the fall pipe.'

'Stranger to you?'

'Absolutely. I thought I had her. I started to ask questions, and she said she'd got into the wrong room by mistake. She came up to me by the door, pleading for me to let her go. That was so as she could have the length of the room for a run at the window. She turned away from me, ran at the window, and dived straight through the opening.'

Martineau was slightly sardonic. 'Which hospital is she in? Or is it the mortuary?'

'Neither. I made a lunge to grab her, and finished up looking out of the window, with my hands on the sill. I saw her turn over in the air like an acrobat, or a high diver if you like, and land on her feet. It must be a fifteen-foot drop out of the window, but there's a patch of weeds which my landlady calls the back lawn. She seemed to land as light as a feather, then she shot out of the back gate and away. She ran like a lad.'

'That takes a bit of believing,' said Martineau. 'You're not trying to kid me, are you?'

'The grass is short at this time of the year. She seemed to land light, but she left her heelmarks all right. They're still there if you want to go and look at them.'

'Mmmm. Had she taken anything?'

'There's nothing missing, as far as I can see. I could see that she'd been looking in drawers. There was my Dad's gold watch, but she hadn't touched it.'

'Do you think she was looking for the ten thousand pounds?'

'I can't think of anything else she could have been looking for. That, or some clue to it.'

'I can't see Costello using a woman for a job of that sort. She must be an associate of Leatherjacket, as you seem to think. Can you give me a description?'

'She was small and bonny. She had a smashing little figure, very trim and fit. She reminded me of a ballet dancer in practice clothes, with her black sweater and grey pants. Her hair was red, a sort of darkish coppery colour. No hat. Don't ask me the colour of her eyes, I didn't notice.'

'Would you know her again?'

'Oh sure, anywhere. I wouldn't have thought she was an associate of crooks. She was dead scared, I think, but she had enough of her wits about her to diddle me.'

'We ought to be able to find her. There can't be so many girls in this district who can turn somersaults in the air. If we get to her, we might get to Leatherjacket.'

Eaglan nodded. 'Yes, you should get her. That ten thousand is getting farther away from me every time I open my mouth.'

'Well, it's your legal obligation to assist in every way to find the owner, isn't it? And when we find him, he might not admit being the owner. It would also be an admission of murder and bank robbery, wouldn't it?'

'I'll look nice giving evidence,' said Eaglan ruefully. 'I'll be talking myself out of a fortune, helping to prove that Leatherjacket is the owner of money which would be mine if it wasn't his.'

'It certainly is a comic job,' Martineau agreed. 'You know, that money simply does not have a *rightful* owner. The original owners, Goosey and his backers, parted with it willingly in a genuine crooked business deal, and got something in return for it. They lost both possession and ownership. They haven't a ghost of a claim, moral or legal, even though they have been deprived of the money they got in exchange. So they are out of it. The bank is out of it, if they were ever in, because they have got their own money back. Leatherjacket received the money in payment for something which was not his to sell, but he had both ownership and possession at the time you compelled him to abandon it. As far as I can see, he is still the owner though you have possession. But he is such an undeserving owner that you might be able to resist his claim on the grounds that he has no more right to the money than you have. If you can resist his claim, you should be able to resist any claim.'

'In the event of any action like that, could a judge make me hand over the money to a deserving charity, or put it in chancery, or anything like that?'

43

'I'm blessed if I know. Did you ask young Slade about that?'

'Yes. He doesn't know either.'

'I wonder if anybody will know. There can hardly be a precedent for a job like this. The whole thing is so far removed from ordinary legality and decency it would make a judge go scatty.'

'There's one party you haven't mentioned. Leather-jacket's pals, the bank robbers. They'll think they have a right to a share of the money.'

'Oh sure they will. But they'll have to keep quiet. When we have them inside, well and truly convicted, they might be able to talk about it. Can you imagine them making a legal claim? It would be laughable.'

'So it does look as if I have as much right to the money as anybody else,' said Eaglan.

'I'm no lawyer, but I would think so,' said Martineau. 'And at least you're not a thief – so far as we know.'

'You wouldn't trust the Archbishop of Canterbury's daughter, would you?'

'Of course not. It's contrary to my training and instinct.'

.　　.　　.　　.　　.

On Friday morning Martineau went to see Clay and told him about the girl whom he had already nicknamed Annie the Acrobat. 'I have Eaglan's statement that he caught her in his room,' he concluded, 'so we can pull her in for interrogation when we find her.'

'She should be easy,' said Clay.

'Yes, but I want her soon. In addition to the usual inquiries I'd like to have half a dozen women police and at least one man working under cover.'

'All right, I'll see that you get them.'

'The women can do it their own way, but I want to choose the man myself.'

'Very well. Go and get on with it,' said Clay.

So Martineau went to see Inspector Farnworth, who was a big, tough, jolly woman. In a brawl she was more than a match for the average man, and she had proved it on a number of occasions. But in the handling of women her supreme talent was the winning of confidence by motherly kindness. Her kindness was genuine, but nevertheless she was regarded as the finest 'conner' of women crooks in two counties.

'Hello, copper,' she greeted Martineau. 'No, I can't lend you anything.'

'Oh yes, you can,' he replied, smacking his lips lewdly. 'I want half a dozen young and innocent girls for my own purposes.'

'Not a chance. I have some who *look* innocent.'

'They'll do fine. I want them right away. Daddy Clay says I can have them.'

Miss Farnworth considered. 'What is it all about?' she asked.

Martineau told her about Annie the Acrobat. 'I want your girls in plain clothes,' he said. 'They'll find her more quickly than a shower of clumsy coppers. I want 'em to nose around girls' clubs, youth clubs, ballet schools, swimming clubs, and any other likely places you can think of. You handle it yourself. Just bring me the girl I want.'

Miss Farnworth nodded. 'Since she's so slippery, my women had better work in pairs. I can put four on the job today, and another two tomorrow. Will that do, your honour?'

'But of course. Many thanks. I'll do the same for you sometime.'

'When I want to find a man? Not likely.'

'Don't you ever give a fellow a chance, you cold, cold woman?'

'I've never met one yet that I couldn't eat for breakfast,' Miss Farnworth retorted in good humour. 'Now scram, and let me get on with your work.'

Martineau scrammed, and went to seek out his under-cover man. The selection had already been made in his mind. His choice was P.C. William Hearn, a young fellow who had been a policeman for one year, in the suburbs. On joining the force Hearn had been made thoroughly welcome by members of the police boxing club. He was an amateur heavyweight pugilist of great promise. Martineau had heard about him, had seen him, and had liked the look of him. Now he asked for the young man's temporary transfer to A Division.

Hearn came. He was a big, brawny, taciturn boy with a fighter's face. But even with a granite jaw, stubby nose, tight lips and eyes which were slits of blue light the lad was not unhandsome. When he came to Martineau he was wearing a sports coat and flannels by no means new, and a clean white shirt. He wore no hat, and his brown hair was neat. Obviously it would never be allowed to grow long enough to fall over his eyes.

'Sit down,' said Martineau, looking at him.

Hearn sat, and waited. His obvious intention of speaking when he was spoken to made the older man smile.

'They tell me you can use 'em a bit,' he said.

'A bit, sir,' Hearn agreed.

'Ever had any offers from professional managers?'

'A few, sir.'

'Were you ever tempted to accept?'

'Not the offers I got. You've got to be near amateur championship class to get a really good offer.'

'I understand that you were in that class.'

'I may be now. I wasn't then.'

'But now you're a policeman.'

'That's it, sir.'

'Do you like it?'

'It's all right. I know I've got to get some service in before I can get anywhere.'

'Do you mean that you're looking forward to the day when you'll be doing something more interesting than walking a beat?'

'Yes sir.'

'Some fellows *like* to be on the beat. Finish on time, less chance of getting into trouble, and all that.'

Hearn's silence was an unspoken opinion of beat work.

'Anyway,' said Martineau, 'you know the language of the boxing game. Where do you come from?'

'Luton.'

'You'll know something of London, then?'

'A little, sir.'

'A Luton boy should be able to pass for a Londoner in this part of the world. I want you to go home and take off that white collar. Wear a polo-neck sweater instead, an old one. Get around the gymnasiums in Granchester, and act like you're looking for someone to fix you up with a battle, for money. Use any name but your own. You're not known around those places, are you?'

'No sir. I have only used our own gym. And I've never had a contest in Granchester.'

'Good. If you actually get the chance of a professional fight, you'll have to scrub round it the best way you can. Don't endanger your amateur status, assumed name or not.'

Hearn nodded, still waiting for the real instructions.

'You're probably wondering what is the purpose of all this,' said Martineau. 'I'll tell you. If you've never been on a murder job before, you're on one now. Is that sufficiently interesting for you?'

'Yes, indeed, sir.'

'You've had the description of the suspect in the Burleigh Street job. Naturally you're looking for him. But you will also be looking for a young woman.'

Hearn took out his official pocket book and laid it on the desk. Martineau had not expected him to be carrying it, because he was not actually on duty. Apparently he had come to the C.I.D. prepared for anything. The chief inspector nodded his approval, and dictated the description of the girl who was alleged to have made such a spectacular escape from Cliff Eaglan's room. Hearn wrote down every word.

'She is suspected of being an associate of the man in the leather jacket,' Martineau concluded. 'Through her we might be able to reach him. Memorize the description and then leave your pocket book at home. Leave your lodgings

47

temporarily and put up in some roughish place nearer town. If you spot the girl, don't approach her. Not as a policeman, at any rate. Try to find out who she is, or where she lives, without being obvious about it. Then get in touch with me. Right?'

'Right, sir.'

'You won't be the only man looking for the girl, not by a score. But apart from some women police whom you're not likely to meet, you're the only anonymous type we will have on the job. Try not to get spotted. If you do get spotted, pack up and come in.'

Hearn's taut lips went a little more taut. To be spotted meant an early return to the beat. He did not want an early return to the beat.

'One final thing,' said Martineau. 'If you are forced into a position where you have to grab the girl or lose her altogether, put her under arrest and wheel her in. Suspicion of breaking and entering a dwelling-house with felonious intent on the afternoon of Wednesday the twenty-second will do for an excuse.'

'Yes sir,' said Temporary Detective Officer Hearn, rising to his feet. 'May I ask a question?'

'Certainly. What do you want to know?'

'I don't want to be missing any points. Is there any particular reason why you expect me to find this girl among a crowd of pugs?'

'Because we have already got people looking everywhere else. Any place where there are rings and parallel bars you might get wind of her. If she's there, you find her and let me know. That's all.'

'If she's there, I'll find her,' said Hearn.

6

EVEN in Granchester, one of the biggest provincial cities in England, there were not many privately-owned gymnasiums. Bill Hearn had heard of only one, but he had heard of it before he ever saw Granchester. Blascoe's Gym was known in boxing circles throughout the country. It was the obvious place for a visiting fighter to go. Bill decided that it would do for him, for a start.

Blascoe's occupied the top floor of an old warehouse in a busy part of the city. It had its own door and stairway, which Bill found at the end of a narrow, shabby cul-de-sac. There was no name on the door, but merely the roughly painted words: 'Gymnasium. Private. Keep out.' Bill went in, and climbed three flights of dirty wooden stairs. At the top of the stairs there was a second door which merely repeated the word 'Private'. Bill pushed it open, and at once his nostrils caught the familiar odour of sawdust, resin, embrocation, sweat and leather peculiar to a school for professional pugilists. This, he guessed, was a meeting place of prize-fighters who could at least fight a little.

He stepped inside and gazed round. The windows were grimy and the walls were a dirty grey in colour. The wooden floor may have been swept from time to time, but obviously it had not been scrubbed for years. All this was bad, but Bill noticed that the unshaded light bulbs hanging from the ceiling were of high power. A man could see what he was doing. And the place was well equipped. There were two boxing rings and a big wrestling mat. There were parallel bars, climbing ropes, rings, punchbags, punchballs and a vaulting horse. On the far side of the big room were stripping cubicles which looked big enough to have their own massage tables, and other cubicles above which could be seen the overhead pipes of shower baths. It was not a show place, but it looked like a good work place for fighters in training.

The place seemed to be deserted, but there was a small partitioned office in the corner nearest the door, and from it emerged a thickset old man in sweater, slacks, and old carpet slippers. His grey hair was curly and still plentiful. He peered with bright eyes out of a face which had been roughly rearranged a long time ago. He approached Bill, and candidly looked him up and down.

'Are you wantin' somethin', boy?' he asked.

Bill looked at him coolly. 'This is Blascoe's, isn't it?'

'Sure it is.'

Bill's reticent glance swept the room. 'It looks all right to me,' he said.

'You shoulda been in this mornin' if you wanted to see somethin',' the old man said, but his tone was appreciably more friendly. 'We're quiet in an afternoon, as a rule.'

'I can come another day, maybe.'

'Sure. Are you wantin' a workout, or a knockabout?'

Bill pretended to be surprised. 'A couple of rounds with you?'

The old pug laughed. 'Give over,' he said. 'I hung 'em up thirty years since.'

'For the time being, I'm just looking round,' Bill told him.

'It costs nothin' to do that, so long as you're in the game. You look like it to me. You're not marked, though. Not even a thick ear.'

'I must be good.'

'Either good or green, which is soon discovered. Where you from, if I'm not rude to ask?'

'The Smoke.'

'A Londoner. Well, they're not all good from there. We got smoke here an' scrappers too. You wantin' a fight?'

'That depends on what sort of money there is here.'

'H'm. You'll have to show some talent before you see any sort of money. You're a likely lad, but can you move?'

'Sure. I've just moved from London.'

'A comic, an' all. We do get 'em. You got a manager?'

'Not at the moment.'

'You'll get nowhere without one. They've got the job taped. You'd better see Conk. He'll be in any minute.'

'Conk? Is he a manager?'

'No! Conk Conquest.'

'Oh yes. I've heard of him.'

'You'd be a funny fighter if you hadn't. He owns this place and promotes all the battles around here. He runs the job, more or less. Runs a lot of other things, an' all.'

'Such as?'

A shadow seemed to cross the battered, honest face. Suddenly the old man ceased to be candid. 'Oh, this and that,' he said vaguely, and changed the subject. 'What do they call you?'

'Cool Kelly,' Bill replied without hesitation. The name came so glibly from his tongue that he wondered if he had read it in a book, or heard it somewhere.

'That's a new 'un to me. Did you give it yourself, or earn it?'

Bill shrugged. 'What does it matter?'

'You're cool enough, at that,' the man admitted. 'My name's Spurr. Nipper Spurr.'

'Pleased to meet you,' said Bill. They shook hands.

The next question came. It was truly artless: curiosity without any ulterior design. 'You'll be known in London, happen?'

'Yes.' It was not a lie.

'What brings you up this way, then?'

'For to admire and for to see.'

Nipper frowned. 'That's a funny way to talk.'

'It's a quotation.'

'Poetry?'

'Yes. I learned it at school.'

'Ah.' Nipper was satisfied. Most of the bruisers he knew had learned practically nothing at school. But it was possible for a lad to have remembered a bit of poetry.

'You sound a bit like a amatchure,' he said.

51

Bill shook his head, and resolved that in future he would speak only in words of one syllable. Any suggestion of intelligence could be dangerous. He offered a cigarette, which was accepted. The two men smoked while Nipper talked about the famous fighters who had used the gymnasium in his time.

The door behind them swung open, and a small, stout man bustled into the place. Bill turned and looked at him, and found himself staring. The newcomer had a face like a caricature. It was a face much thinner than faces normally seen on top of stubby bodies. The nose and chin were somewhat like an unequal pair of pincers, and the nose itself was enormous. Obviously this man was Conk Conquest, and the nickname was not in deliberate alliteration with the surname. He wore an expensive velour hat on the back of his head, and Bill wondered what he would look like without it.

Conquest said: 'Morning all.' He gave Bill one brief, shrewd glance, and walked with short, brisk strides into the little office. Nipper hurried after him, and the two men went out of sight behind the partition. Bill pondered whether he would go or stay, and eventually moved to the vaulting horse and sat swinging his legs.

Conquest's business in the office did not take many minutes, and probably it was no more than a check on the takings. He emerged, followed by Nipper. He was making for the door when Nipper said: 'This is the Cockney lad I was tellin' you about. He knows poetry.'

'What does he want?' came the question, just as if it had not already been asked in the office.

'He needs a manager.'

'He needs his head seeing to, if he wants to be a fighter.'

Bill dropped from the vaulting horse. 'You can talk to me like that when I owe you something, not before,' he said.

The promoter answered with good humour. 'Take my advice,' he said. 'Look at Nipper here. He used to be a bruiser, and not a bad one either. Look what it got him. And look at that mug of his.'

'I could have another hundred battles an' still be better lookin' nor you,' retorted Nipper.

'Ah, but I've got the brains,' said Conk. 'You never had enough sense to tell the time, only when a referee was counting it for you.'

The exchange of insults was made with a false acrimony which amused Bill. He guessed that it was part of a regular cross-talk act. The two men were associates of long standing, and probably old friends.

'Don't be a fighter, lad,' said Conk. 'Go and get a job shovelling coal. You'll be better off.'

'Do you say that to all the boys?' Bill wanted to know.

'I do. All the time.'

'What if they all started taking your advice?'

'They won't, lad, they won't. They all think they're going to be the best there ever was. It makes no difference if they get battered till they're cross-eyed.'

'Take no notice of him,' said Nipper. 'He'll break your heart before you start. There's fame an' fortune to be made in the boxin' game.'

'You see?' said Conk. 'You can't cure 'em. This silly old has-been still dreams of glory. He hasn't enough sense to walk across the road. It's what they made pedestrian crossings for, for fellows like him. He's not fit to be at large.'

'Always discouragin' folk, that's what you are,' Nipper accused.

Conk ignored him. He was considering Bill. 'How much fighting have you done?' he asked.

'A moderate amount.'

'How many victories?'

'Quite a number.'

'Helpful, aren't you? *Where* have you fought?'

'Nowhere, under the name I'm using now.'

'You changed your name and came to the North? Why?'

'I thought I'd have a fresh start.'

'It's no good if you're barred under some other name.'

'I'm not barred under any name.'

'What's up, then? Police after you?'

Bill appeared to hesitate, then he said: 'Don't be so bloody insulting.'

Conk nodded grimly and turned to go on his way, a busy man again. 'If he wants a fight he'll have to have a manager,' he said to Nipper. 'Tell him to see Jack Briggs. Jack could do with some new cannon fodder.'

The door banged, and Conk was gone.

'There's a man who could make you a champion,' Nipper said proudly. Then he added cautiously: 'If you got it in you, that is.'

.　　.　　.　　.　　.

Bill went to Blascoe's gymnasium on the following morning, which was a Saturday and a fine one. He thought that half-past ten would be a good time to arrive, a time showing not too much eagerness or energy without being too late to miss anything of importance. The gymnasium was well patronized, as might have been expected on a Saturday. Both rings and the wrestling mat were occupied, each with a number of spectators, and most of the other equipment was in use. Nipper Spurr was not in sight, so Bill looked into the office. Nipper was writing laboriously in a ledger. He glanced up as Bill's face appeared at the edge of the doorway.

'Hello, lad,' he said. 'Come in.'

Bill entered, and Nipper saw the small gladstone bag which he was holding. 'You've brought your stuff,' he said with approval. Then he said: 'You've brought it on the wrong day. This is our busy time. Most of the boys here are members, and week-ends is the only time some of 'em can get a bout.'

'Never mind,' said Bill. 'I'll leave the bag in the corner there, if I may.' He knew that there was nothing in the bag which would betray him.

'Aye, put it down,' said Nipper. He was looking eagerly thoughtful. 'We *might* be able to get you a knock,' he murmured, and Bill knew that his willingness to do that was

54

inspired merely by his curiosity. He wanted to see how the
big stranger would shape in the ring.

'We haven't all that many heavyweights,' he continued.
'If Eddie Ellam comes in, he might be glad to have a go
with somebody his own size.'

He resumed his book-keeping. Bill dropped his bag in the
corner and went out into the gymnasium to watch the
bouts. He did not know how much he would eventually
have to pay for the use of the gym's amenities, and he was
content to wait until this matter was mentioned to him.
It would go on his expenses sheet, anyway.

For a few minutes he watched two middleweights pound
each other with more enthusiasm than skill, but his attention was not wholly given to the men in the ring. The
spectators interested him, too. They were a mixed lot. The
pugilists, youngsters and veterans, were not difficult to
identify. Others, sharp-eyed impassive men, were not so
easy to place. Some appeared to be prosperous, while some
were definitely shabby. There might have been managers,
trainers, bookmakers or sports writers among them and there
certainly were impecunious hangers-on of various sorts.
There would be one or two men with police records, Bill
guessed. Like horseracing, the business of prizefighting has
its criminal element. Boxing matches are attended by a
certain amount of betting. Where betting regularly occurs,
there are crooks.

Then he heard the voice of Nipper beside him, and Nipper was saying: 'Here a minute, Eddie.' He turned, and saw
a man as big and muscular as himself.

'This is Eddie Ellam,' said Nipper. 'Eddie, this boy calls
himself Cool Kelly.'

Ellam seemed to be about thirty years of age, but was
probably a year or two younger. He was, therefore, a boxer
of considerable experience. But he was not badly marked, a
fact which led to the presumption that he had some skill in
defence. Bill had never heard of him, so it was probable that
he enjoyed only local fame. The reason for this would show
itself in the ring, no doubt.

'How d'you do,' said Ellam, as they shook hands. 'You must be a stranger. I know every heavyweight in these parts.'

'He's a Londoner,' was Nipper's interjection. 'He'd like a knock-about with somebody.'

Over Nipper's head the glances of the two big men met. Bill gave a slight nod. 'All right,' said Ellam. 'Put us down.'

Nipper became excited. 'Ten minutes,' he said. 'You can go and strip.'

Fifteen minutes later every person in the place was standing around the ring where Bill faced Ellam. It did not matter that Bill was a stranger, it was the eternal attraction of the heavyweights, the big fighting animals. They met in the middle of the ring with the merest touch for a hand-shake, and then each man was behind big eight-ounce gloves which seemed to make two impenetrable barriers. Bill had adopted a stance which was slightly different from his usual one, because he did not wish to be spotted immediately as an amateur. He crouched with his left foreshortened, and he felt oddly confident in the new position. He felt like a professional.

Bill has his own plans about this sparring match. His pride would not allow him to make himself appear to be incompetent but, assuming that he would be able to make a show against Ellam, he would not make too good a show. He wanted to appear as a hopeful youth with a little talent and a lot to learn. By doing so he would not be badgered by any manager, and yet he would still be accepted at the gymnasium.

Ellam's skill ruined the plan. He tried Bill with a few feints, then he attacked. He was quick and tricky, and he scored points. In coping with him, Bill instinctively showed the quality of his own ringcraft. The murmur of the crowd held a note of approbation.

It was a genuinely friendly bout, and neither man was trying to hurt the other. The ability to put an opponent down with either hand was Bill's greatest pugilistic asset, and now as he dealt 'love taps' he wondered how much punching power there was in Ellam's fists. Could the inability to 'punch his weight' be the reason why this accomplished boxer was not famous?

Before a halt was called, Bill was quite sure that he knew one reason why Ellam had never been a champion. The man was not as good as he looked. He used his repertoire of professional tricks too lavishly, and before gloves were finally lowered he had begun to repeat them. Bill was sufficiently skilful to perceive and remember them. A situation developed where he could have counter-punched drastically had he wished. His growing superiority was perhaps not apparent to the crowd, and he did not want it to be. But he became moderately certain that he could thrash Eddie Ellam in a real fight.

It was evident that Ellam did not think so. He was beaming with satisfaction. He came to Bill's corner and spoke in friendly and patronizing tones. 'That was great, kid,' he said. 'You're just the boy to get me in trim. We can have lots of goes. It'll be good for both of us.'

Bill said: 'Sure,' and then he was aware of a sudden silence among the nearest spectators. He looked up and saw a pair of cool, considering eyes behind a huge nose. Conk Conquest was at the ringside, and those round about were waiting to hear what he had to say.

'Very pretty,' the great man said with sarcasm. 'Clean and clever. A couple of fairies bashing one another with buttercups.'

There was a general snigger. Bill grinned, but Ellam flushed and frowned. 'That's not fair, Mr. Conquest,' he complained. 'It was only a tap-tap. You could see I wasn't trying.'

'I could see *somebody* wasn't trying,' said Conk, and his glance held Bill's for a moment before he turned away.

7

On Sunday morning Bill went to Blascoe's gymnasium again. There were a number of people in the place when he entered, but he could see nothing of Eddie Ellam. He was not displeased about that. He did not want to spar with Ellam too often if the discerning – and, perhaps, suspicious – eyes of Conk Conquest might be watching. He stripped, and knocked a punching bag about for a little while. He was drumming a punchball when Nipper Spurr approached with a big, ungainly young man of twenty or so.

Nipper's manner convinced Bill that Conquest had been talking, to Nipper at least, about yesterday's bout with Ellam. Nipper was almost respectful, a man asking a favour.

'Kelly,' he said. 'Have you time to give this boy a turn with the gloves on? He's a lad who's a trier, an' he wants some experience.'

Bill looked at the lad who was a trier, and met a glance of beseeching innocence. This was a lamb *asking* to be led to the slaughter. It was impossible to refuse. 'Sure,' he assented.

'Get stripped, Micky,' said Nipper briskly. And as the youth dashed away to the dressing rooms: 'Mike Farrell they call him. Don't hurt him.'

Bill discovered that Farrell was a novice who had never had a professional fight. Because of this there were no spectators except Nipper. The bout became a boxing lesson, with Nipper supplying the advice and Bill demonstrating what would happen if the advice were not immediately taken. Thus Nipper would say: 'If you don't keep that right elbow down you're goin' to get one between wind an' water . . . Like that.' Farrell was not a very apt pupil but as Nipper had said he was a trier. Moreover he was grateful. As he and Bill went towards the showers after the bout his spaniel eyes were almost worshipful. 'Thanks, Kelly,' he said. 'Thanks a load. Gosh, you're good, aren't you?'

Bill perceived that here at least there was one person whom he could question with safety, though he was not hopeful of learning much from such an innocent. He reflected ruefully that Farrell would do to practise on, having not the faintest notion that he had met the one man who would tell him what he wanted to know.

'Been coming here long?' he began, casually enough.

'No,' was the reply. 'Only a few weeks. Since I came out of the Army.'

'National Service?'

'Yeh. They started me off boxing and I did all right. I thought I'd follow it up.'

Bill was disappointed. 'You won't know the blokes here very well, then,' he suggested.

'Oh yes I do, some of 'em. I've known old Nipper practically all my life. He's been here for donkeys' years, you know. I used to come here when I was a kid, with Matt Spurr who was my playmate. When there was nobody about Nipper used to reckon to teach us to box.'

Bill was still not interested. 'Was this Matt Spurr some relation of Nipper?'

'Grandson. Nipper always fancied making him into a scrapper, but I don't think he had it in him, to be honest. Besides he was too little. Sable had more about her nor him.'

'Sable?'

'Yeh. Sable Spurr. Funny name, isn't it? She's Matt's sister. A bit of all right, an' all. I used to fancy her but she was a year older and she said I was only a kid.'

Bill began to have a hope. The granddaughter of a man who looked after a gymnasium was a promising subject of inquiry. 'Did she used to come in here as well?' he asked.

'When we were kids? Yeh. She kept it up longer nor us, an' all. She's a wizard acrobat. Or at least she used to be.'

Bill wondered if Mike could hear his pulses hammering. He hoped that his colour was all right, and he strove to control his voice. 'She sounds all right,' he said. 'I like a girl who can do something. What's she like to look at?'

'She's a smashing little redhead. Ginger for pluck, they always say. She looks after the house for Matt an' Nipper, an' has a good job an' all. Secretary to an antique dealer what goes all up an' down the country buying antiques.'

'Mmmm,' said Bill with mild interest, while he wondered if he was letting this talk about strangers go on for a suspiciously long time. He looked at Farrell. The young man was staring into space, probably seeing a mental image of Sable Spurr. He suspected nothing. No doubt he thought that a fellow patron's interest in the gymnasium keeper's family was quite natural.

They had entered the stripping rooms, and they were in adjoining cubicles. They could converse without raising their voices from the normal.

'What happened to the generation in between?' Bill asked.

'Eh?'

Bill cursed himself for forgetting his one-syllable rule. 'What happened to Sable's father and mother?'

'Her father was killed in the war, and her mother died. Cancer.'

'Oh. Are you and this Matt still pals?'

Mike's voice became slightly hesitant, then all at once he was a young man of character and reserve. 'We don't see each other much, these days,' he said. 'Since we've both been in the Army we seem to have gone different ways.'

Bill thought that he detected a note of disapproval. He switched back to the safer subject of the girl. 'Sable Spurr,' he said. 'She sounds like a racehorse.'

'Well, she's a thoroughbred,' came the warm reply.

Bill's retort was apparently made in jest: 'Since you're out of the running you'd better give me her phone number.'

'They don't have a phone,' Mike answered seriously. 'They live in the same little house in Rochester Street where they've always lived.'

He went into the showers then, and began to sing with nasal sentimentality. Bill showered quickly and quietly, and

60

was soon out of the stripping rooms. He looked for Nipper, and found him involved with another old-timer in an argument about the respective fistic abilities of Jack Johnson and Joe Louis. He realized that this was no time to engage Nipper in talk about his grandchildren, but he lingered, one of the debaters' grinning audience, until Mike emerged and saw him thus lingering. After that he chose his moment to saunter out of the gymnasium and go in search of a public telephone box.

Sunday is traditionally the Weekly Rest Day of the majority of C.I.D. men, but with a murder job on his hands Martineau was on duty. Bill's call was put through to his office. He answered promptly. He had been waiting too long, in his opinion. It was time that one of his many scouts chipped in with some news.

'Hearn speaking,' said Bill. 'I may have got something, sir.'

'Let's hear it,' was the terse order.

'A man called Nipper Spurr looks after Blascoe's Gym. He lives in Rochester Street with two grandchildren, Sable Spurr and Matt Spurr. The girl, Sable, will be about twenty-one or twenty-two years old. She is a small redhead described as a smasher, and she is a first-class acrobat.'

'Good man,' Martineau's voice was warm. 'Sable Spurr. How do you spell it?'

'Your guess is as good as mine, sir.'

'What is this Matt Spurr like?'

'I couldn't push the thing too hard. All I got about Matt was that he was young and on the small side, and has done his National Service. I didn't get the number of the house, either.'

'We'll get that from the Burgess Roll. You've done very well indeed. Have you been twigged yet, do you think?'

'No sir. I've been very careful.'

'Very well. Continue as before, and spend as much time in Blascoe's as you can. You may learn something else. Leave the girl to me, now. If you see her, she'll probably have a policewoman on her tail. If you see Matt Spurr and you think he's Leatherjacket, bring him in.'

.   .   .   .   .

According to the Burgess Roll, the family of Spurr lived at number 30 Rochester Street. The house was one of a row of similar houses in a smoky working-class district. The neighbourhood was poor but respectable. Both sides of the street had the same sort of houses, and at first number 30 looked like an impossible subject for prolonged observations. But reconnaissance revealed that there was a dye works with a high clock tower in the next street, and in the back street, behind the house, there was cleared land which was used as a parking place by people who worked in the vicinity.

The manager of the dye works was quite willing to help the police, and very soon there was a plain-clothes man behind the highest window of the tower. He was equipped with field radio and binoculars, and he could look down over the roofs of one row of houses and see the front door of number 30. The back of the house was observed from plain C.I.D. cars, which used the parking place in relay at irregular intervals. These arrangements would not be necessary during the hours of darkness, when the house could be watched more closely by men lurking on foot.

Martineau himself waited in a car which was tucked away in an opening near the dye works. With him were Devery and Cassidy, and Cliff Eaglan. It was hoped that Eaglan would be able to identify Sable Spurr when she appeared. In the event of his doing so, policewomen in plain clothes would shadow the girl wherever she went, and would themselves be followed by detectives who would be able to assist them if required to do so. Martineau hoped that Sable would lead him to her brother. He had sound reasons for believing that the brother was no longer living at number 30.

He freely discussed those reasons because they were not yet established facts, about which he would have to be reticent. 'Assuming that Matt Spurr is our friend Leatherjacket, there'll be others besides the police who want to talk to him,' he said. 'More than one man was needed to do the Northern Counties Bank job. Somewhere there will be two or three hard nuts who want an explanation. Matt will be keeping out of their way. Either he robbed them, or he lost their money when he was on an errand for them. I'm of the opinion that he robbed them. He has no police record, and the other bank robbers probably have records which are long and bad. He was less likely to have the police nosing around his place, whereas they might have expected to have to stand a search. He was the logical choice to hold the money till it cooled off.'

'With many threats as to what would happen to him if he didn't play it straight,' said Devery.

'Of course. And now that the money's gone, he'll be remembering the threats.'

'I wonder if they've talked to the sister, to get her to tell them where he is.'

'How can they, without taking the chance of giving themselves away? They're more likely to watch her, or the house, as we're doing. I rather thought we might see somebody around Rochester Street when we cased it the first time, but there was nobody.'

'Another bit of no luck for Inspector Pearson.'

'Yes. He's recovered the bank's money and he's got Goosey Bright who won't talk. Now he's got Matt Spurr as a suspect and that's as far as he can go. He's not getting anywhere trying to find Goosey's backer.'

'Who rented the warehouse to Goosey?'

'Both the warehouse and the office we found are supposed to belong to the Ashley Property Company. It isn't registered at Bush House, has no telephone number, and has an empty office in Sawford for an address. A man has been seen there once or twice, calling for letters. He has one of the finest vague descriptions I've ever heard: "Medium height, medium build, medium colouring, unobtrusive clothes, age between thirty and forty-five". Pearson is waiting for him to call again. What a hope!'

'It'll be somebody who can't talk because he doesn't know, or won't talk because he daren't.'

'I suppose so,' Martineau agreed. He reflected that the business of waiting, of keeping observations, was the most tedious part of police duty. But he was hopeful. He had an inside man at Blascoe's Gym, a detail ready to follow Nipper Spurr about, and a more elaborate detail to keep track of Sable. At the moment he could do no more. He lit a cigarette, stretched himself as well as he could in the car, and looked at his watch. 'The pubs are open in ten minutes,' he said. 'Heigh-ho, this is a dry job.'

'It's making a mess of my Sunday,' said Eaglan without rancour.

Martineau was about to reply when another voice forestalled him. It was the man in the tower, almost immediately above the car. The slight crackle of his walkie-talkie made his utterance seem to be excited. 'Attention,' he said. 'FR One speaking. Are you receiving me? Over.'

There was the voice of Headquarters. 'GCPR One. We are receiving you. What about the Chief Inspector? Over.'

'I can hear,' said Martineau. 'Over.'

FR One gave his information. 'The front door of number Thirty has been opened. An elderly man and a young woman have emerged. The man has closed the door, and he appeared to try it to make sure it was locked. He is wearing a blue suit and a grey trilby; is of medium height and broad-shouldered. The woman is wearing a light natural-coloured coat, light-coloured shoes, no hat: is medium height or a little less, normal figure, auburn hair. They are walking away together, in the direction of Derbyshire Road. Message ends. Over.'

'We have received your message,' said Headquarters. 'Over.'

'Message received,' said Martineau.

Devery had started the car. As it nosed out into the street and turned towards Derbyshire Road a group of four young people, who had been standing apparently in conversation, began to break up. Two girls began to walk briskly in the same direction as the car, and two men stood looking after them. When the girls were some distance away the men exchanged a word, and began to stroll after them.

Driven slowly, the car was nearly at the junction with Derbyshire Road when an old man and a red-headed girl crossed in front of it. 'That's her, all right,' said Eaglan as the girl glanced at the car. 'That's the lass who dived out of my window. I'd know her anywhere.'

'Good,' said Martineau, and he looked at Devery.

The car stopped at the main road. Devery put head and arm out of the window and looked back. One of the fast-walking girls raised her hand in a casual salute. Devery's arm was out as if in an exaggerated turning signal, but his forefinger was pointing at Nipper and Sable Spurr, who were about to pass out of sight of the following policewomen. His signal was acknowledged.

Martineau sighed. 'That's it, then. Drop Cliff wherever he wants to be, and then we'll get back to Headquarters.'

Eaglan asked to be dropped in the centre of town. The policemen obliged him in this matter, and Martineau thanked him. Then Martineau said: 'Stop at the Ring o' Bells. We have time for a pint.'

They were back at Headquarters in time to wait for the first report about the movements of Sable and Nipper. When it came, Martineau took it himself. 'Proceed,' he said to P.W.17 Browne.

'Six fifty-eight, took up observations on subjects designated,' said Policewoman Browne. 'They walked along right-hand side of Derbyshire Road towards the centre of town. Seven five, they stopped and entered the Elite Snack Bar, and immediately emerged. Seven twelve, they entered the Napoli Coffee Bar and emerged. Seven seventeen, they stopped and had a short talk outside the Garter Inn. The man entered, while the woman waited outside. He emerged after one minute. Seven twenty-two, the man entered the Cazalet Club while the woman waited outside—'

'Just a minute,' said Martineau. 'Have they been in and out of pubs and clubs the whole time?'

65

'Yes, sir. And they're still doing it.'

'Do you realize that in any one of those places they can make brief contact with somebody and pass on a message?'

'I do indeed. But there's nothing I can do about it.'

'Either they've done that, and are covering their tracks, or they're simply looking for somebody. Are you sure you haven't been spotted?'

'I'm as sure as anybody could be in the circumstances.'

'Mmmm. Very likely they're simply searching for somebody. All right, never mind reciting the rest of it. Carry on with the job and ring me again in half an hour.'

'Verygoodsir,' said Policewoman Browne.

The chief inspector sat in thought for a minute or two, then he picked up the telephone and made the first move to obtain a search warrant for the premises of number 30 Rochester Street. He also arranged for a search team to be ready. Then he waited for the next report.

Punctually it came. 'From the time of the last report,' began the policewoman. 'Seven thirty-eight, the subjects entered Chan's Chinese Chophouse and emerged immediately—'

'Hold it,' said Martineau. 'Have they been in and out of places the whole time since you last reported?'

'Yes, sir.'

'And nothing else of note has happened?'

'Nothing has happened, sir.'

'Very well. Bring the girl here to me. Suspicion of breaking and entering a dwelling-house, afternoon of Wednesday twenty-second April, if she won't come willingly. Bring the old man if he's willing, but if he objects, let him go. Get a car laid on, and pick them up as quietly as you can.'

'Verygoodsir,' said Policewoman Browne.

8

SABLE and Nipper were brought to Headquarters without trouble, Nipper insisting that he must accompany his grand-daughter even before he was asked to do so. Martineau decided to interview them separately, and he had the old man brought to him first. Having had occasion to call in at Blascoe's Gym at various times in his career, he knew Nipper, but did not know anything to his discredit. He was inclined to believe that the old pugilist was as honest as the day, but, in the light of sad experience, he was not going to be surprised if his inquiries proved that there had been a fall from grace.

'Now then, Nipper,' he said, smiling but not rising to offer his hand. 'How are you?'

'I'm as right as I ever was, Mr. Martineau. What do you want with my grandchild?'

'Which one are you referring to?'

Nipper blinked. 'I mean the girl. Our Sable.'

Martineau indicated the chair facing his. 'Sit down and we'll talk about the other one. The boy. Your Matt.'

Nipper's mounting uneasiness was visible. 'Is that what you want Sable for?'

'Mostly, yes.'

'Has the lad done summat?'

'We don't know. We're trying to find out.'

'What do you think he's done?'

'Shot and killed two men.'

Nipper rocked as if he had taken a hard punch. 'So that's it,' he muttered. 'Oh dear, oh dear.'

'Did you suspect something of the kind?' Martineau asked gently.

'There were nowt to suspect. Only . . .'

'Only what?'

'Nothin'.'

'The boy has left home, is that it?'

'You'll get to know that. Yes.'

'Did he tell you he was going?'

'No.'

'When did he leave?'

'Wednesday night, early on we think.'

'Was that after he'd seen the *Evening Guardian?*'

'I don't know. I was at the gym.'

'But you do have the "Guardian" delivered to your house?'

'Aye.'

'Did he take any luggage?'

'Not as we know of.'

'He just walked out and didn't come back?'

'That's it.'

'Had you any warning of this? Had he said anything at all?'

'Not to me he hadn't. Not a word.'

'Had he said anything to anyone else? Sable, for instance?'

'I don't know. I don't think so.'

'So you went looking for him this evening.'

'Yes.'

'Did you see anything of him?'

'No.'

'Any of his friends?'

'That's just it. We don't know his friends. He doesn't talk about 'em.'

'Didn't it occur to you to tell the police he was missing?'

Nipper's glance did not quite meet Martineau's. 'No,' he said. 'We never thought on it.'

Martineau was easy and affable. 'All right, Nipper. We'll do our best to find him for you.'

'It isn't for us you'll be findin' him.'

'You could be right. By the way, that's an odd name,
Sable. A nice name, but unusual. How did she come to be
called that?'

'Her mother was half French, an' when she was born her
hair was a light sandy colour. Well—'

'Stop! Let me show my profound learning. I think I see
it. *Sable*, pronounced sarble, is French for sand. As simple
as that!'

'That's it. Her mother used to stroke her head an' call her
Petite Sableuse, which is about the only French I know. But
now everybody calls her Sable, the way it's spelt.'

'Mmmm. Remarkable. Now you'd better leave me while
I have a word with her.'

'I'd sooner stop, if you don't mind.'

'Sorry, Nipper. It would be better if you didn't stay.
Don't fret yourself. I give you my word that she won't be
bullied.'

Nipper nodded, and reluctantly departed. Sable was
brought in, and Martineau politely got to his feet. He
looked searchingly at the girl. She was worth looking at. A
little smasher, as the man had said. Hair like burnished
copper in a shady room, and eyes like topaz in sunlight.
A lovely face, and the figure of a ballet dancer. A little
beauty.

'Do sit down, Miss Spurr,' he said. 'I hope we don't have
to keep you so very long. I presume that you know why
you're here?'

The girl sat down. She was agitated, and obviously
striving to be calm. 'I'm not sure that I know,' she said.

'There was been an allegation that you climbed into a
bedroom at a house, number forty-four Lonsdale Road,
during the afternoon of Wednesday the twenty-second. The
natural inference is that you went there to commit a felony.
But you don't *look* like a common thief. If you can give me
any other explanation which is reasonable, I might be
prepared to believe you.'

'I didn't go to steal,' the girl said desperately.

'Then why did you go?'

'I – I can't tell you.'

'Did you know the man whose room you entered?'

'No.'

'Did you know *of* him?'

'I'd heard something about him, yes.'

'And in consequence of what you had heard about him, you went to his room?'

'Yes.'

'What had you heard about him?'

'I can't tell you anything more.' The girl's eyes were wild, and her voice had risen to the ragged edge of hysteria.

'Steady now,' said Martineau. 'Do you smoke? Here, have a cigarette. Let us see if we can talk about this thing without getting upset.'

Sable accepted the cigarette gratefully. She smoked, and seemed to become normal. Martineau smiled at her. 'That's better,' he said. 'Now you look like the girl who had the nerve to dive head first through a bedroom window.'

She smiled faintly in reply, and remained silent. Martineau saw something in the smile. 'You think I'm trying to gain your confidence with a cigarette, don't you?' he said. 'You're quite wrong. I'm merely trying to *give* you the confidence to listen to me and answer my questions sensibly. Don't you trust the police?'

'Well, nobody does, do they?' she replied with the hint of a shrug.

'You'd be surprised. Have you ever had anything to do with the police before?'

The girl shuddered. 'No, never.'

'But you've heard people talk.'

'Yes.'

'When a man has been caught doing something wrong, to excuse himself to his friends he's got to say that the policeman is a liar. It happens all the time.'

She was suddenly thoughtful. He nodded. 'Somebody might have spoken on those lines to you, recently,' he said.

'Maybe. Don't policemen ever tell lies?'

'They tell as many lies as other people, but very rarely under oath. It does happen, but not often. Would you believe me when I tell you that I am being absolutely honest with you now, and that I shall continue to be honest?'

For a long moment Sable sat in thought. Then she said: 'Yes, I think I do believe you.'

'Very well. At the moment I am investigating the death of two men, by shooting with a pistol. The crime appears to be murder. There may be circumstances which will reduce the crime to manslaughter, or there may be circumstances which will lead to an acquittal on the grounds of self-defence. The first is possible, and the second is highly improbable. But at the moment it is a murder job which also involves bank robbery. Is that quite clear?'

'Yes.'

'All right. Now we will go back to where we were before. You entered a bedroom in Lonsdale Road by climbing in through the window. How did you know you were in the right room?'

'There was a framed picture of the Granchester Police football team on the wall.'

'So you knew that the occupant was connected with the police?'

'Yes. He's a detective.'

'He is not a detective. He left the police some time ago.'

The girl stared. 'Oh dear,' she said.

'Who told you about him? Your brother?'

'I won't answer that. You can't make me.'

'In a way you have answered. But don't worry, you haven't betrayed your brother. When he sent you to get something from that ex-policeman's room he betrayed himself. I shall get to know all I want to know. You won't be able to avoid telling me, and it won't be your fault. You played your part, but he had already lied to you, hadn't he?'

Sable shook her head. 'I don't know,' she whispered.

'His act of running away makes you doubt what he told you?'

'No. That could go with the story. It's something else.'

'His story could still be true?'

'It could be, yes. It could be true about the part that matters.'

'And what part is that?'

'The shooting.'

'I see. And do you think it would be to your brother's disadvantage if you told me what his story was? I may be able to find out the truth of it. I assure you I have no intention of charging an innocent man with murder.'

Sable considered that. 'I don't see how it could hurt him for you to know what he told me,' she said at last. 'It makes all the difference, that man not being a policeman. He could be a crook, couldn't he?'

'It is possible,' Martineau agreed.

'You see, Matt thought it was police corruption. He *said* he thought it was police corruption. He said that there might be a lot of policemen mixed up in it, and he was afraid they were going to blame him for something he didn't do. You see, he was coming from a place with a suitcase which a friend had asked him to deliver to another friend. It had a suit of tails and a white tie and a shirt and stuff in it – the case I mean – because this friend was an entertainer who'd got a posh booking and he was borrowing the tails. I asked Matt what time this was, and he told me, and I asked him what he was doing at a friend's house so late. Then he admitted he'd been to a gambling house again, after he'd promised me he wouldn't go any more.'

'I can see how that reluctant admission strengthened the story in your mind.'

'Yes, it did. Anyway, he said he was in Burleigh Street, and he saw this detective called Eaglan, talking to two more fellows. He said none of them noticed him at first. A fight started, the other two against Eaglan, and he pulled out a gun and shot them both. When he'd done that he looked round and saw Matt, and he tried to shoot him because he was a witness. But his gun jammed or something, and he couldn't shoot. Matt ran away and Eaglan chased him, and he had to drop the suitcase or else be caught. He got away, but Eaglan got the suitcase. Matt was afraid they'd trace the case to him and then blame him for the shooting. A lot of detectives plotting together could easily do that.'

'And that was Matt's story? Where did he get the idea that Eaglan was a policeman?'

'He used to go with a girl who lives in Lonsdale Road, straight opposite to where Eaglan lives. She pointed him out to Matt, and told him his name. And of course Matt thought he was still a policeman.'

'That's reasonable enough. But why bring *you* into it?'

'Matt said Eaglan was a big brute and he was scared to death of him. He was afraid of what he would do to him if he caught him. Also I'm a better climber. We went and looked at the house. Matt kept at a safe distance and I climbed in at the back.'

'Were you badly scared when Eaglan caught you?'

'I was at first. Then I could see he wasn't going to hurt me. Not right away, anyway. He didn't look like a murderer. I thought he looked nice.'

'So you made your excuses and left.'

The girl smiled faintly. 'That's one way of putting it,' she said.

'So you went back to your brother?'

'Yes. I told him what had happened. I said I'd seen a leather suitcase, but not an old fibre one. He asked me if I had looked in the leather case, and I said I hadn't had time.'

'How did he receive that?'

'Oh, he was badly worried. We went home and I started making the tea. I heard him get the paper when it came, and I thought it was natural he'd want to read it. When we were having our tea he was so sort of preoccupied I don't think he knew what he was eating. I said then that Eaglan didn't look like a murderer, and he said he was like a lot more coppers, hand-in-glove with crooks and setting up jobs for them. That's what he said. He must have believed it.'

'Some people find such things easy to believe,' said Martineau. 'Did you talk about anything else?'

'No. I was washing up after tea, and I heard him go out. He didn't say where he was going. I haven't seen him since.'

Martineau refrained from asking Sable for a description of her brother. His men would get that from the neighbours. And if there was a photograph of Matt at number 30 Rochester Street, his men would borrow it for reproduction. 'Does Matt have a leather jacket?' he asked.

'Yes. He wears it a lot. Oh dear, I'm so worried about him.'

'I'd like to tell you not to worry, but I'm afraid he's in real trouble,' said Martineau gently. 'You must be prepared for that. I'm very much afraid that the story he told you won't stand up to a thorough inquiry. Still, the inquiry will be made. You can rely on that.'

'What about me? Am I in trouble for climbing into Eaglan's room?'

'I think you can forget about that. Obviously you had no felonious intent. There is a technical matter of trespass, but nobody is going to bother about it.'

'Then can we go now, Grandad and I?'

'Yes, you can go. And remember, what you have told me has served to clear you of complicity in a crime, but it hasn't got your brother any deeper in trouble than he is already. When you get home you might find that somebody has been in the house. Policemen, searching with a warrant because we have to be absolutely sure that Matt isn't at home. If you find that a picture of him is missing, don't worry. It will be returned to you tomorrow.'

'Oh,' the girl said. 'Oh, you're hunting for him, aren't you? I didn't realize. Oh!' She burst into tears.

Martineau let her weep. While he was waiting, a slip of paper was brought and placed before him. It told him that the search of number 30 had yielded nothing of importance except a photograph signed 'Love, Matt,' of a

74

young man in Army uniform. There was also a description:
'Height 5 feet, 6 or 7 inches; well-built but slim; bushy hair,
brown with a little red in it; brown eyes; clean shaven;
aged twenty-one years; may be wearing brown leather
jacket.'

Sable was still weeping. Martineau scribbled instructions
at the foot of the paper: 'Copy picture. Description Express
Message All Districts, wanted for interview.'

9

ON Monday morning Bill Hearn 'rang in' for information.

'Yes,' Martineau told him. 'We found the girl. We watched her and Nipper for a while. They were seeking the brother, Matt Spurr. So I had them in and talked to them. Apparently Matt had told the girl a tale to get her to search Cliff Eaglan's room for that suitcase. Both she and Nipper are on the level, I think. But you must keep on hanging around Blascoe's. You might hear something else, or you might be able to lay hands on Matt if he tries to contact the old man.'

So Bill returned to the business of pretending to be an aspiring prizefighter. He went to the gymnasium. He thought that he would still be secure in his false identity, and he was likely to become more secure as time went by. It was not probable that Nipper would be telling the world – and certainly he would not be telling Mike Farrell – that he and Sable had been in the hands of the police. Mike had no means of knowing that police action had been a result of conversation with Bill, and Nipper had no knowledge of the conversation.

On that Monday morning the gymnasium was quiet, as Bill had hoped. He had purchased a morning paper, which he was carrying unopened in his hand. Looking into Nipper's office to pass the time of day, he noticed that the old man had a paper spread on the desk before him. He sat down casually on a stool in the corner nearest the door, and unfolded his own paper. The description of Matt Spurr was on the front page.

Bill read a news item about the exorbitant transfer fee of a famous footballer, and commented upon it. Then he read the Matt Spurr report.

'I say,' he said. 'The coppers are wanting a lad called Spurr, something to do with those two fellows who were shot. No relation of yours, Nipper?'

'Only grandson,' Nipper answered seriously, but he did not seem to be particularly depressed. He was not a man who could go on worrying for ever.

'Oh dear,' said Bill, and then he was tactfully silent.

'I think he's got into bad company just lately,' said Nipper. 'He's been led away by somebody older.'

'It says here they want him for an interview. Perhaps he's only a witness.'

'Happen so.'

'What does he do for a living?' asked Bill, to keep Nipper on the subject.

'He was a warehouseman up to a month ago. A cotton warehouse, handlin' bales of stuff.'

Again Bill thought it better to be silent. Nipper answered his unspoken question. 'He's got the sack,' he said. 'He had words wi' the foreman. Been unemployed since.'

The gymnasium door flew open, and Eddie Ellam rushed into the place. He made straight for Nipper's office. 'I say, what about young Matt?' he demanded of Nipper.

'You know as much as I do,' the old man replied.

'He's got in with a rough lot, hasn't he?'

'I tell you I don't know.'

Ellam perceived that he was forgetting to be sympathetic. 'Well, I hope it turns out all right,' he said. 'Happen it won't be so serious after all. How's Sable taking it?'

'She's gettin' used to it, same as me.'

'Mmmm. These things happen. If there's anything I can do to help, let me know.'

'I don't see as anybody can help much,' said Nipper, but he was thoughtful. 'Do you happen to know a feller called Eaglin or Eagling?'

Ellam shook his head. 'I can't seem to bring such a name to mind,' he said. 'What does he do?'

'I don't know. But he was a bobby not so long ago. In the detectives.'

'I know a D or two. I can ask about him. What is it you want to know?'

Nipper shrugged helplessly. 'That's just it. I don't know *what* I want to know. I'm wonderin' if I could find out anythin' to help. I don't even know whether he's a good man or a bad 'un.'

Ellam snorted. 'What, a copper? Give over! What's he got to do with it, anyway?'

'I'm not tellin' you that. Happen I shouldn't a-mentioned it at all.'

'Where does he live, this ex-D?' Ellam persisted.

'I don't see as there's any need for you to know that.'

'You're among friends, you know.'

'Aye, happen I am.'

Ellam laughed. He was about to say something when Bill interrupted. 'We've got company,' he said, rising to his feet.

He was instantly attracted to the girl who had entered the gymnasium. Like some other big men he admired small, perfectly made women. Her hair, eyes, and face were wonderful, he thought. He was entranced by the way she walked. Sable Spurr, of course. And Martineau had given his opinion that she was honest. Bill was immensely pleased about that.

Sable came to the office. 'Hello, there,' Ellam said in welcome. She smiled and answered, and glanced at Bill, who had not ceased to look at her. Then she said to her grandfather: 'I left my key at home. Can I have yours?'

Nipper gave her a latchkey. She thanked him and said: 'Mr. Mason has had to go to York, and he won't be in again today. So I'll be at home if you want me for anything.'

She gave Bill another quick glance as she turned away, and he received the impression that she was curious about

78

him for some reason. When she was on her way out Ellam called: 'Chin up, Sable,' and she turned and waved to him with a small, serious smile. Then she was gone.

'What a job the lass has got,' said Ellam. 'A day off every time the boss goes out of town.'

'She's done well, and she'll keep on doin' well,' said Nipper with quiet pride. 'She's a good 'un.'

'Do you want to have a bit of a bash?' Bill inquired of Ellam.

'No, Kelly, this morning I can't,' Ellam replied quickly. 'I got some business. I just called to leave my bag, 'cause I'll be coming in this afternoon.'

He moved the bag to the far corner of the office and made his departure. On the way out he passed Conk Conquest coming in. Conk's arrival was a signal for Bill to get out of the office. He spoke to the newcomer and said 'Cheerio' to Nipper. On his way out he let the gymnasium door bang behind him so that it bounced a little. He held it open that little way and stood listening. Conk was the only man he had any worries about.

He had missed some opening remarks, but he heard Conk say: 'Have they been asking you about it?'

'Eddie has,' Nipper replied. 'He was right nosey.'

'What about Kelly?'

'He just asked me if Matt was any relation, that's all,' was Nipper's answer.

Bill quietly closed the door and went just as quietly down the stairs. What he had overheard made him think that Conk was inclined to be suspicious, but how seriously inclined he could not even guess.

When he reached the street he looked for Ellam's stalwart figure, and on perceiving it he began to follow. He had decided that the veteran heavyweight was worth following for either of two reasons. Ellam had left the gymnasium in a hurry after being rather curious about an ex-policeman called Eaglan. That was one thing. The other thing was that he might be following Sable Spurr.

Ellam was not a difficult subject for observation. He was

easy to see, and he did not look back. It was soon quite obvious that he was not following Sable. He was looking for somebody, and eager in his quest. Bill dogged him to a flat above a restaurant in All Saints Road, to the County Sporting Club, to a bookmaker's office, to one and then another block of offices which housed a number of firms, and to a restaurant where morning coffee was being served to smart women and business types. The hour of eleven came and passed, and then thirty minutes later the public houses were open. Ellam went to the Northland Hotel and entered.

In the bar of the hotel Dixie Costello and his lieutenant, Ned Higgs, were at that early hour the only customers. They were in conversation with Ella Bowie, the barmaid. As Ellam entered the bar and approached the group, Dixie frowned. 'No, Eddie,' he said, before the pugilist could speak.

Humiliating are the obligations of economic need. For that anticipation of a request Ellam could have banged Dixie's head on the bar. As it was, he did not even show displeasure. 'Can you spare me a minute, Dixie?' he pleaded. 'I think I've got something for you.'

Ella Bowie immediately moved to the other end of the bar. Dixie sighed, bored with the story before he had heard it. 'What is it?' he asked wearily.

'I know you must be interested in the Burleigh Street do, on account of who got killed.'

'In a way I'm interested,' Dixie admitted.

'You know the coppers are seeking a kid called Matt Spurr. Well, I've been talking to somebody very close to him.'

'Don't be vague. I don't want half a tale. The name, man.'

'Nipper Spurr, his grandfather. He don't have any parents.'

'I don't think Nipper knows much. What does he say?'

'He was asking me if I knew a fellow called Eaglin or

Eagling, who used to be on the police, C.I.D. He don't know the man himself, you understand. I said I'd help him to find out whatever it was, and what was it anyway. When I showed a bit of curiosity he closed up, and wouldn't even tell me whereabouts Eaglin lived.'

'Huh. Is that all?'

'Yes, that's all.'

'They're looking for the character who did the job. What can this Eaglin have to do with it?'

'I dunno. I just thought it might be a clue for you.'

'A clue to what?'

Ellam shrugged, and remained silent. Dixie looked at him for a moment, then he put his hand in his trousers pocket and pulled out a big wad of one-pound notes. He extracted one note from the wad and put it on the bar in front of the other man. 'That's more than it's worth,' he said. 'But I'll see you right if there should happen to be something in it.'

'Thanks, Dixie,' said Ellam as he pocketed the note. He was disappointed with the reception of his news and with the reward.

He was turning away when Dixie said: 'Eddie.'

'Yes?'

'You seem to think you know something. Take a tip from me, and don't go showing any more curiosity. Just keep your nose out of things, see? You'll not be forgotten if there is anything.'

'Righto, Dixie,' said Ellam humbly, and he departed.

'Cliff Eaglan,' said Higgs. 'I know him. He got sacked off the force for belting a sergeant on the nose. He was lucky they didn't have him up for it.'

'Do you know where he lives?'

'No, but it's the easiest thing in the world for me to find out. Some of his old mates will know his address. I'll get it this afternoon.'

'You do that,' said Dixie.

Outside the hotel, a little way along the other side of the street, Bill Hearn watched from a shop entrance. Through

81

two panes of glass he saw Ellam emerge and walk away. The man's whole demeanour had changed. He no longer had a purposeful air, and he seemed somehow to be smaller. His search was over, Bill guessed. He had made contact, and now he would be going home for his midday meal.

Bill looked speculatively at the Northland. On an old envelope he had made a note of each of Ellam's calling places, but this last place could be remembered without a note. It was known to every adult person in the city. Somewhere within its walls was an associate or friend of Ellam's, of an importance sufficient to warrant a tiresome search. Bill pondered for some time, and finally decided to go into the place and have a look round.

Ellam had gone into the hotel by the front door, so it was improbable that he had been in the 'vaults', where the roughest, poorest people were wont to gather. It was likely that he had made his contact in a front bar. Bill went in, and wandered into Ella Bowie's bar, where he ordered a bottle of beer.

Costello and Higgs were still there. They did not appear to notice Bill. He looked them over. He thought that they were a little too flashy to be ordinary business types, and too natty to be 'class'. He could not place them. He had heard of Dixie Costello but he did not know him. And he was not thinking about Dixie just then. He drank his beer, and went to look in the other public rooms of the hotel. He saw nobody who seemed likely to have been Ellam's contact. He went out, reflecting that the two men in the bar were the likeliest clients. He was complacent in his assumption that they had not noticed him. He had the makings of an excellent policeman, but he was still very young.

As soon as Bill walked out of Ella's bar, Ned Higgs said: 'Twig the boy?'

Dixie nodded. He said: 'Two outsize sweaters, one following the other.' He pondered, and because he knew almost everything about the small, shady world in which he moved he said: 'Conk said something about a new heavyweight spending a lot of time around Blascoe's Gym. A promising lad who doesn't put everything in the shop window. He could be a copper, and that boy could be him. We'd better have some inquiries made.'

'I'll see to it, Dixie,' said Higgs.

That afternoon Bill reported to Martineau. The chief inspector listened without interruption to his story of the morning's work. He concluded: 'I made a list of all Ellam's calling places.'

'Put them on a report and submit to me,' Martineau told him. 'They may come in useful, if I'm guessing right. Now, which bar in the Northland was it where you saw the two flash types? Was the barmaid a good-looking blonde with a scar on her face?'

'That's right, sir.'

'The fellows were both in their early forties? Medium height, well built, and hard looking?'

'Correct.'

'H'm. Were you wearing a sweater?'

'Yes sir. As directed.'

'Did either of them see you?'

'I don't think they did. They never looked my way at all.'

'And you were the only other customer?'

'Yes.'

'That sounds bad. They saw you all right, and pretended not to. I believe they were Dixie Costello and one of his mob. Dixie would be the one Ellam wanted to see. He's as sharp as a fox. He might be asking questions about you this very minute. You will have to be very much on the alert, and prepared for anything.'

'Yes, sir,' said Bill, realizing that it had been a mistake to follow Ellam into the Northland wearing a sweater. 'I'm sorry. I'll stay on my own pitch in future.'

'No. You made a small error of judgement, but don't let it cramp your style. The policemen who never make mistakes are the ones who never do anything at all. Carry on as before and take all legitimate chances. But henceforward be on the lookout for trouble.'

'Very well, sir. Any news of Matt Spurr?'

'Not a whisper,' said Martineau.

Bill went on his way and tried to keep his mind on his work. But thoughts of the job in hand always ended by involving Sable Spurr. Bill wondered if she would visit Blascoe's Gym again, and how soon. He mentally rehearsed conversations with her, and he imagined situations in which he appeared favourably in her presence.

10

TEN thousand pounds was an important amount of money even to a wealthy gambler like Dixie Costello. He was accustomed to big gains, which he took as his right, and he had been known to be philosophical about heavy losses. The occasions for such resignation had been infrequent, and the attitude only adopted when every possible effort to retrieve the losses had been made. It followed, therefore, that if Dixie had lost any money in the affair which had involved the shooting of two of his henchmen, then he was going to get it back if he could.

But to be ruthless and persistent in his attempts to get his hands on ten thousand pounds, Dixie did not need to have suffered a loss. In his code of ethics, something for nothing for Dixie was sound, legitimate business. If a large sum of money was in need of an owner, then it seemed to be entirely right for Dixie to have it. And if someone else should succeed in acquiring the money, then Dixie would quite sincerely consider himself bereaved.

This Divine Right of Dixie went even further. Dixie could do no wrong. If – as the police suspected – Dixie had had an interest in the buying of stolen currency, then it was his own greed and treachery which had resulted in both old and new notes being lost to him. But Dixie would not look at the business that way. He would not blame himself. He would blame two men – now dead – who had bungled the job. He would also blame a character called Matt Spurr for having the effrontery to ruin the Dixie plan by defending himself and his money. He would also blame a person as yet unknown – this Eaglan fellow, was it? – for interfering and taking possession of the money.

Ten thousand pounds was a big enough sum to bring

Dixie down from the heights of his own self-esteem and actually do something himself, personally. It was not yet the time for dealing out rough treatment, he coolly surmised. There would have to be some intelligence work: he had to find out who possessed the money, and where it was kept. It was not work which he could leave to a mutton-headed subordinate. His own wits and something which he called his prestige were needed.

So, on the evening of the day when he had first heard the name of Eaglan, Dixie submitted himself to the indignity of waiting for somebody. He waited in Lonsdale Road, in a black Ford Zodiac with both front windows down.

At seven o'clock Cliff Eaglan emerged from his lodgings and walked towards the nearest bus stop. Somebody not far away began to whistle 'Lonely Footsteps'. Dixie started the car and drove along until he was ahead of Cliff, then he stopped the car at the kerb. When Cliff drew level with him he leaned towards the near-side window and called: 'Your name Eaglan?'

Cliff stopped. He peered, and saw that there was only one man in the car. He also recognized the man. 'Yes,' he said. 'I'm Eaglan.'

'My name is Costello, Dixie Costello. You may have heard of me.'

'I've heard of you. What do you want?'

'I want to have a talk with you.'

'What about?'

'Oh, this and that. All quite friendly. Not terribly busy, are you?'

Cliff pondered briefly. It seemed obvious to him that Costello was now openly joining in the game for the ten-thousand-pound kitty. That being the case, he would have to be encountered at some time or other. At the moment he was offering to meet on equal terms. If the offer was refused there would still be a meeting, with a less friendly approach and with no equality at all.

'No, I'm not busy,' Cliff admitted. 'I was just going to the pictures.'

'Get in the car, then. We'll go and have a jar somewhere. I won't keep you long.'

Cliff got into the car. 'Which pub?' he asked.

'Any old pub,' said Dixie cheerfully. 'You name one.'

They went to a small, quiet local inn called the Fleece. The place was aptly named for the scene of a conference with Costello, Cliff reflected ruefully. But Dixie did not appear to see any significance in that. He did not have that sort of brain. A name was just a name to him.

So early in the evening the inn's little bar was deserted. The two men sat at a table in the corner. Cliff accepted a half-pint of bitter and Dixie had a glass of whisky, a small one.

'How are you doing since you packed up the force?' Dixie asked, when the landlord had served them and moved away.

'Not so bad.'

'Ever regretted it?'

'Oh yes. I did at first. Now, I'm not so sure. I got the sack, you know.'

'Yes. You snottered a sergeant, didn't you? My oh my! Clouting a police sergeant is something I've dreamed about for years.'

'I shouldn't have done it. I lost my temper, that's all.'

'Don't we all. But you'll be all right, kid. I can't see much in the copper job myself.'

'It's the same as anything else, it's a good job if you like it.'

'Fair enough. How did you come to meet Sable Spurr?'

Cliff took time to think before he answered. When he had identified Sable for Martineau, the chief inspector had not discussed the girl's character with him because he had never met her and knew very little about Sable except that she was the sister of Matt Spurr who was wanted on suspicion of murder. He considered the advisability of telling Dixie anything about her, and could not make up his mind.

'I met her by accident,' he said.

'Where?'

'We'll leave that for the moment. How does she come into anything?'

Dixie smiled. 'We'll start afresh,' he said. 'I'll tell you one or two things I know. I don't think the girl matters: she was just an opening gambit. To begin with, the police don't have that ten thousand nicker that was advertised. Somebody else has it.'

'Mmmm. That's interesting. Who told you that?'

'All the police aren't dumb. There's one or two who can talk. And I have lots of ears to listen.'

'Yes. I'd heard that you had one or two contacts inside the force.'

'What Dixie doesn't know isn't worth knowing. I had inquiries made about *you* this afternoon. You've been in and out of the copper shop quite a bit lately, and you've been going around with Martineau. You're the boy who picked up the money, aren't you?'

Cliff could see no good reason for denial of the suggestion. If he wanted this crook to believe him at a later time, when the affair might have developed into something hectic, he would have to tell the truth at the beginning. 'Yes, I picked it up,' he admitted.

'Then, if the police know that, why don't they have the money?'

Cliff explained to the boss mobster the rudiments of the law regarding found property.

'So you hung on to it. That was smart,' said Dixie in a tone of genuine congratulation, the effect of which was somewhat spoiled by the sudden predatory gleam in his eyes. 'Where is the money now?'

'In a safe deposit.'

'Which one?'

'The Gibraltar. I don't think anybody will crack that one.'

'I think you're dead right. But as the temporary owner you can get it out, can't you?'

'No. To cover my responsibility I insured it, and the

88

insurance people tied the job up properly. I had to tell them that it wasn't actually my own money, you see. They weren't going to accept the business at all, at first. They made it safe. When that money comes out of the Gibraltar it'll happen in the presence of a shower of officials of different sorts. The insurance people aren't taking a chance on me changing my mind and skedaddling with the lot.'

'Are you telling me the truth?'

'Go to the Centurion Insurance Company and ask them. Tell them I sent you. Or ask Martineau.'

'I wouldn't ask that bastard the time of day. What does he think about you having the money?'

'He's got over it. I don't think he's bothered, now.'

'Do you think you'll get it, sometime?'

'I don't know. If I can have the use of it for a while I'll be happy.'

'Why, what would you do with it?' asked Dixie, slightly amused, slightly mocking. Happiness of that sort for Cliff Eaglan was not included in his programme.

'It's a business,' Cliff explained. 'I think I could get it at a reasonable price, and I *know* it could be made into a gold mine.'

'What sort of a business?'

'Radio. The owner is getting on in years, and he's ready for retiring.'

'Old Isaacson?'

'Yes,' said Cliff. A refusal to answer would not have prevented the other man from ultimately knowing.

'I agree with you. At the right price it would be a good buy. I might buy it myself.'

'It would need too much of your attention.'

Dixie grinned. 'It wouldn't if I had a smart, keen lad like you running it for me. Salary and commission.'

'That wouldn't do for me,' Cliff answered firmly. 'To go all out, twelve to fifteen hours a day, I'd want a share. A partnership.'

'I don't care much for partners. They're a nuisance.'

Cliff shrugged. 'Too bad.'

Dixie looked at him curiously. He said: 'Being an ex-copper, you'll know a bit about me. Would you work for me – or *with* me?'

'I'd work with anybody if it was honest. After the lawyers had made it airtight.'

'Airtight, eh? Well, I never did care for a fool. Happen we can talk about it seriously sometime. Just now, I want to know more about this unclaimed money. Matt Spurr is the rightful owner, you say?'

'There's nothing rightful about it. I believe he's the *legal* owner.'

'When the police pick him up, can he claim the money?'

'If he chooses.'

'And if he don't choose?'

'Providing there is no other claimant, it remains in my possession.'

Dixie was bland. 'And suppose you get run over?'

'I thought of that possibility. If anything happens to me, the money remains in my estate until legally claimed. My solicitors are well briefed about that.'

'Don't they get their money if you don't get the ten thousand?'

'Certainly they do. But they're interested in seeing what will happen. A job as totally twisted as this is something new to them.'

'Tell them not to worry. *Your* lawyers won't be in it at the finish.'

Cliff did not reply. Dixie continued, a man with as much knowledge of criminal law as a policeman, asking simple questions to get an ex-policeman to talk. 'What do you think will happen to young Spurr when they catch him? Will he get topped?'

'He committed a double murder, and he did it with a gun. That's a hanging job on two counts. But though he was presumably on unlawful business he was defending himself against attack, and there was no premeditation. I don't think they'll hang him. I don't think public opinion would stand for it.'

'I'm with you there. He'll get a long piece in the nick.'

'If they convict him,' said Cliff, and then he bit his tongue.

'What do you mean by that?'

'Well, *I* don't know what evidence the police have got, do I?'

The mobster's eyes narrowed. 'They've got you,' he said. 'You were Johnny-on-the-spot.'

Because he did not know what subsidiary plans Costello had made to help in achieving the ultimate object, Cliff felt himself to be on dangerous ground. If Dixie wanted to be absolutely certain that Matt Spurr would not be hanged, he would not scruple to do away with an eye witness. He would commit murder by proxy for a much smaller sum than ten thousand pounds. But, while Cliff was the one who could identify Spurr as the gunman, he was also the one who could save him from the hangman. He decided to take a chance on that. He preferred to tell the truth, anyway. Telling lies to Costello was even more hazardous – indeed, far more hazardous – than lying to the police.

'Yes, I was on the spot,' he admitted. 'I'm also the man who can testify that Spurr was acting in self-defence.'

'Tell me the whole thing from the start,' Dixie invited.

Cliff told him.

'So that's where the sister comes in,' the other man commented. 'The police got on to Spurr through you telling them about her high-diving act.' His tone became mildly contemptuous. 'What were you trying to do, talk yourself out of ten thousand nicker?'

'I was trying to be on the level, that's all.'

'All right, try to be on the level with me. You seem to be middling good at the law. How does Matt prove he's the owner of the money?'

'He proves he had it before I got it, and I corroborate that. It goes against the grain, but I can't see how I'd benefit by lying. I don't know what will become of the money, but if ever it becomes mine it will be partly because I've told the truth about it all along.'

'So Matt proves he had it. Don't he have to prove where he got it?'

'Not necessarily. If he declares that it was freely handed to him in exchange for something, that will have to be accepted unless there is evidence to the contrary.'

'If somebody comes along and says it's theirs, and that he stole it, what then?'

'It will have to be proved,' said Cliff. He grinned faintly. 'It would need a damn good story, so late in the day.'

'Somebody could have his reasons for not coming forward right away.'

'Maybe. Why are *you* so interested?'

'I'm always interested in money.'

'I see. Well, now you've got everything I know about the job. Have we anything else to talk about?'

'Have another drink. I've got to think about this, and I might as well do it here.'

'As you wish,' said Cliff. He allowed Dixie to pay for another round, since the party was for his benefit.

Dixie thought, and did not appear to solve any problems. At length he said: 'You've talked to Martineau. Has he mentioned my name in connexion with the job?'

'He may have done, with Kaplan and Ray being friends of yours. But I don't recollect him saying anything important.'

'You seem to tell him everything. Will you be telling him about you and me having a chat?'

Cliff had already thought about that. He had expected the question, which was nothing more than a veiled threat. There was no sense in antagonizing Dixie for nothing. Also, he was not obliged to confide everything to Martineau, since Martineau did not confide in him. The interview had merely strengthened his own surmises about Dixie, and Martineau had already made the same surmises.

'No,' he said. 'I won't say anything to Martineau, unless one of his men has seen us together.'

'Nobody has seen us together, kid, except the landlord here. And he's not interested.'

'That's that, then. But I suppose Martineau will have an idea or two about you.'

'Oh, naturally. He's had ideas about me for years, but it hasn't done him any good. He's a proper bugbear. If anything happens anywhere in the town, he thinks it's me.'

'And isn't it?'

Dixie grinned. 'Not often,' he said.

II

On Tuesday morning Bill Hearn went to Blascoe's Gymnasium as usual. He found Nipper Spurr there, and four youngsters who were all of lightweight physique and all comparatively unmarked. He said: 'Good morning, all.' None of them returned the greeting. Nipper looked at him stonily. The others exchanged secret, sheepish grins.

So it seemed to Bill that Conk Conquest's suspicions had hardened. He had talked to Nipper, and Nipper had been talking to the boys. Bill remarked coolly: 'Quiet this morning,' and turned away. As he did so, the door opened and Eddie Ellam appeared with another man. They could have been only a few yards behind Bill when he entered the gymnasium.

Ellam flung a general greeting to all present, but he looked at Bill. He was smiling, but there was an irrepressible gleam in his eye which Bill did not like.

'Hello there, Kelly,' he said. 'I've been telling a friend of mine about you, and he wants to meet you. He's hoping you'll have a knockabout with him. Help him to get back to form.'

Bill looked at the man whom Ellam called a friend, and reflected that if he had never seen a plug-ugly before, he was certainly seeing one now. It was a man in his early thirties, a heavyweight not so tall as Bill, but phenomenally broad and powerful. He had a Hogarth face, battered, brutal, coarse and cunning. His bullet head was surmounted by dirty ginger bristles. He looked as if he measured more round the neck than the head.

'On my left, Cool Kelly,' said Ellam with almost open mockery. 'On my right, Barney Slatters.'

Slatters showed tobacco-brown teeth as he shook hands.

94

Bill also smiled. Both smiles were as false as instant mutual dislike could make them.

The name was familiar to Bill. He had seen it in the newspapers, and he had heard it mentioned in police circles. Slatters had been the most promising heavyweight which Britain had seen in years. Here at last, the sports reporters had said, was a fighter who might win the world title. But Slatters had bad blood in him. When he had money – and he would not consent to its being withheld and safeguarded – he sought the drink and the women. The drink made him ugly and vicious. He marred his career, and then he ruined it. He killed a man in a quite unofficial brawl, and he was convicted for manslaughter. The case was a bad one, and the sentence was ten years imprisonment. Since emerging from prison he had lived by 'borrowing' small sums from people who preferred to lend rather than incur his enmity. The police knew how he lived, and they were waiting for somebody to make a complaint. But Slatters did not utter threats, or press anybody too hard. Prison had taught him that much caution.

Bill wisely thought of refusing to go into the ring with the man, but grinning faces made him think again. Because he was a policeman, it had been arranged that he should have a thrashing or be shown up as a man who was afraid to go into the ring with Barney Slatters. He decided to take a chance on the thrashing.

'I'll be ready in five minutes, trunks and sweater,' he said, and went off to strip.

In the stripping room he thought about the chance he was taking. He knew that he was an amateur ready and able to bid for the national championship, and that was something which his opponent would not know. He also knew that there was a vast difference between an amateur champion and a professional fighter such as Slatters had been in his heyday. In his heyday. Nearly ten years ago. A ten-year sentence with remission meant seven-and-a-half years of forced abstemious living with limited exercise. They had been followed by two years of ease, with immoderate participation in all the vices there were. No training at all, probably. Bill began to wonder why he had hesitated to fight.

At the ringside one of the lightweight boys laced his gloves, and then he slipped through the ropes to face Slatters. There was of course no referee, and no time-keeper. Bill decided that if his opponent disregarded the rules, then so would he. He adopted the upright stance of the amateur, with his left hand ready for swift attack or defence. If the attitude would give his antagonist the impression that he was a novice, all the better.

Slatters shuffled into action in characteristic style. He crouched with head low and both hands high. His body seemed to be unguarded, but Bill was not deceived. The way he was standing, he was a hard man to hit.

He bored in, trying to get to close quarters immediately. Bill's left fended him off. This was the pattern of the first few exchanges, with Slatters trying to fight, and Bill keeping out of serious trouble while he took the measure of his opponent. He was surprised. Slatters's famous right hand was as ponderous as a windmill sail. He was still a deadly puncher, but he had lost the lightning speed by which he had made his reputation. In the first minute Bill tapped him in the vicinity of the eyes a few times, and received two hard lefts to the body. But he managed to avoid the right.

The match went on in this fashion until the sweat began to run into Slatters's eyes. He was slightly out of breath, too. Still Bill remained on the defensive. He had to cope with a number of dirty tricks, but he did not allow the other man to get close enough for his tricks to be dangerous.

Then Slatters caught him with the right. It was a very low blow which might have crippled him, but he was turning and he took it on the hip bone. It was so hard and hurtful that he was temporarily lamed. He would have been in serious trouble then if Slatters had not been out of breath. He hopped around until the other man held up both gloves, palm outward.

'Time,' he said. 'Round One.'

Bill went to his corner knowing that he had been hit with a glove which was loaded with lead. That was the explanation of the comparatively slow right hand. As he rested, favouring his left leg, a deep anger began to burn slowly in him. A man as strong as Slatters with a leaden fist could cripple a man permanently, or crush his face until he was unrecognizable. So that was the intention, not merely to humiliate but to mark for life. Bill's anger grew. He looked for Nipper, to see, if he could, what that old sportsman thought about the intended massacre. He was rather surprised to find that Nipper was not at the ringside. He looked towards the office, and was even more surprised to see the old man peep round the doorpost at him. 'Something queer going on,' he mused. Then he saw Slatters grinning wickedly at him, and he forgot about Nipper.

It did not occur to Bill to call off the fight and demand to see Slatters's right hand. The heat of wrath in his brain gave him other ideas. He called: 'Come on now,' and left his corner. Slatters came to meet him, breathing more easily now but still sweating profusely. Bill did not wait even the fraction of a second. He abandoned his amateur stance and went in low and fast. Slatters was really surprised, and more unprepared than he ought to have been. A hard, foul right caught him in the abdomen. The sickening blow made him temporarily unable to retaliate. Bill was under his guard and pounding him even more hurtfully in the region of the solar plexus, and the frontal muscles of his body were not in condition to take such punishment. Instinctively he covered up, but he did not receive an instant's respite. Bill raised his sights and smote him on the left ear with sufficient force to shake his brain. This was followed by a stunning blow on the other side of his head. Dazed, and for the time being unable to breathe, he was helpless. His head came up as he gasped for air. Quite merciless, Bill hauled off and delivered the hardest blow of all, to the side of his jaw. He staggered back to the ropes, then fell flat on his face.

The bout was over. As Bill was turning away he looked over the awed faces near the ring and caught a flash of movement near the door. He had one glimpse of a brown leather jacket before the door closed. In an instant he was through the ropes and running towards the door. As he ran he tugged with his teeth at the laces of his right-hand glove. In sweater and trunks, with short socks and ring boots, he hardly considered himself to be dressed for the street. But that did not matter. The gloves did matter. How could he arrest a man while he was wearing eight-ounce boxing gloves? Certainly he could beat his captive into submission but, with a man only half his size, such an assault might mean that he would be deprived of his prey by an angry crowd.

The leather jacket was out of sight more than one flight down, when Bill reached the top of the stairs. He went down two at a time, no longer tugging at the glove. The street door was hinged to close itself by its own weight. In his haste Bill stepped outside and allowed the door to slam. Near the end of the alley a young man heard the sound, and looked back. Bill saw a startled face and a shock of hair, a leather jacket of a style not frequently seen in England, grey flannel trousers and scuffed shoes with thick crêpe soles. The young man vanished into the street, running.

Bill sprinted to the end of the alley and looked along the street. The man whom he supposed to be Matt Spurr was turning another corner thirty yards away, entering the busy main street of Bishopsgate. Bill went after him. Soon after reaching Bishopsgate he saw him dash into a big public house called the Flying Horse. On the assumption that Spurr would run straight through the place and out by the back door, Bill turned along the side street to the inn and ran round to the back. There was a door in a backyard, but nobody in sight. He ran on, and found another door on the further side. If Spurr had come out by that door without being delayed inside the building, he had gained at least thirty yards.

Bill went on until he was in Bishopsgate again. He stopped, looking for Spurr, but he failed to see him. Then he turned back and entered the Flying Horse.

Beyond an inner door there was a lounge bar. Four customers, all men, were present. There was also a middle-aged barmaid who was still sufficiently concerned about her appearance to have her hair bleached to a flaxen hue. A derisory grin began to grow on her face as she looked at Bill and his boxing gloves.

Bill was too preoccupied to be upset by derision. 'A chap in a leather jacket came in here a minute ago,' he said. 'Where is he?'

'He ran straight through and out the side door,' the woman replied. And one of the customers asked: 'What's up? Has he pinched yer Lonsdale Belt?'

Bill turned, frowning. Suddenly apprehensive, the man found something to look at in his glass of beer. Bill went and stood over him. There was a rather tense silence until he said: 'Unlace these gloves, will you?'

The man unlaced the gloves in silence. Then Bill asked: 'Is there a public telephone in this place?'

'Just outside the door there, in the lobby,' the man said.

'I need to make a call, and I haven't any change with me.'

The man took a handful of change from his pocket. He proffered four pennies. 'Thanks,' said Bill. 'If you're not here when I come in again, I'll leave it with the barmaid.'

'Don't bother, lad,' he was hastily told. 'Don't bother.'

He went into the lobby and telephoned Headquarters, deeming it better for the neighbourhood to be searched by a number of men than by himself alone. He gave the news of Spurr's whereabouts to a police telephone operator, together with a description of the clothes he was wearing. Then he asked to be put through to Martineau.

Though it was not Bill's normal time for making contact, he was again fortunate enough to catch Martineau in his office. 'Is something the matter?' the chief inspector asked.

'Yes sir,' Bill said. 'I've been rumbled.'

'Too bad. No rough stuff, I hope.'

'They sent a fellow called Barney Slatters to trounce me in the ring. I came out of it without getting hurt.'

'Well done. Slatters used to be very good indeed. I expect

99

it was Dixie Costello who fluffed you. He can smell copper anywhere, and all the *eau de cologne* in the world won't put him off. He probably had you investigated after you showed yourself in the Northland. Is there anything else?'

'Yes,' said Bill with calm bitterness. 'I saw Matt Spurr this morning, and let him slip me.'

Martineau was equally calm. He said: 'Tell me about it.'

Bill told him, and he listened without comment. 'Well,' he said when the story was ended. 'At least we know what Spurr is wearing. I'll send a couple of men to Blascoe's, to see if Nipper will spill anything.'

'What do *I* do now, sir?'

'You seem to be the sort of fellow who gets into things. You can go back to your regular lodgings, but I'll keep you in plain clothes for a while. Report to me when you've done your flitting and had your lunch.'

'Very good, sir,' said Bill, relieved that he would not yet have to resume duty in uniform. He walked out of the Flying Horse in a better mood. He had seen Matt Spurr and he would know him again. He was staying on the job. He still had a chance of making a name for himself.

He went back to the gymnasium and climbed the stairs. The door at the head of the stairs did not yield when he pushed it. He pushed harder, and assured himself that it was locked or barred. His anger returned. Lock him out without his trousers, would they? He pounded on the door, but there was no answer. At last, thoroughly roused by what he considered to be an act of petty spite, he backed off and ran at the door with his shoulder. The door flew open, and he stood surveying the room beyond. He saw Barney Slatters sitting on a stool at the ringside, holding his stomach and looking sick. Nipper, Ellam and the four lightweights were standing near him, staring at Bill in the doorway. Their expressions differed. There were various degrees of dislike, and there was a sort of shame. There was also respect.

Bill walked across and stood in front of Slatters, looking at him. 'How is he?' he asked, of nobody in particular.

'A bloody copper,' said Ellam. 'Let's set about him.'

Bill looked at him, and at the others. He swung his boxing gloves by the laces, as if he were tempted to hit somebody with them. He grinned.

'Yes,' he said. 'I'm a police officer. I've just been on the phone, too. A few of my mates are on the way here, to see what they can find.'

'Dirty spy,' said Ellam, but not very loudly.

'I'm spying for the law. I am *not* spying for a filthy spiv, like you're doing,' said Bill directly, and Ellam was silent under the speculative glances of the others.

Bill went to the stripping rooms. He had a shower, and dressed himself without haste. He packed his kit, and walked out swinging the bag. On the way to the door he looked once at Nipper, and Nipper avoided his glance. He did not look at any of the others. Ellam shouted something after him as he started to go down the stairs, but he could not hear what it was and he did not trouble to go back and ask.

12

THE bed-sitting room was fairly large, having been the second bedroom of a house which was built in spacious days. The flowered wallpaper was of excellent quality. It was begrimed by the sooty atmosphere and it showed the stains of a generation of careless occupancy, but it was still intact upon the walls. The carpet had been worn threadbare, but its pattern was still discernible. The single armchair was shabby, but it was comfortable. The bedstead was a horrible arabesque of brass and iron, but the bed was comfortable, too, and wider than most.

The girl who lay on the bed was young and of full shape. Her hair was crisp and dark, her lips were full and red, and her cheeks were rosy. In a few years she would be blowzy. She wore a crumpled cotton dress and smoked a cigarette, and gazed mockingly at the young man who was sitting in the armchair.

The man in the armchair was Matt Spurr, and he also smoked a cigarette. He stared at the fireplace with its unlit gas fire, and frowned in bitter thought. He had been sitting there alone since noon, with his back to the window and afraid to go near it, waiting for the girl to bring him something for his lunch. She had arrived twenty minutes ago, at five o'clock, smelling strongly of liquor and carrying a squashed pork pie in a brown paper bag. She had spent the entire afternoon drinking, first in a public house and then in a club. 'With friends,' she had deigned to explain.

That, he thought, is what happens when a man is hunted by the police. Anybody can tread on him. This girl had him quite literally at her mercy. She could betray him at any time. She would do so when she grew tired of having him in her room, and that would be when he had no more money to give her. The need for money had sent him to his grandfather that morning, and his narrow escape had shaken his nerve. Sitting there alone during the afternoon, feeling shamefully treated by the girl, his thoughts had turned more than once to the possibilities of the gas fire. It could have put an end to his troubles, but he had been deterred by the thought that nobody but his sister and his grandfather would miss him. Most people would say 'Good riddance'. The girl whose gas fire he used would revile his memory for getting her into trouble with the landlady.

No, no suicide. He would show them. They would talk about him as the one who had got away with thousands. He would go and take that money from Eaglan at gun point. Maybe tonight, maybe tomorrow. He would have to think of a plan for getting into Eaglan's room. He wouldn't muff it as Sable had done.

The girl interrupted his reverie. She said: 'You never told me how much you got from your grandad.'

He did not look at her. 'I'm not going to tell you, either,' he said. 'That money may have to last awhile.'

'While you sit there on your backside, doing nothing?'

'You don't understand. I've got to figure things out.'

'I understand, all right. Whoever this bloke is who's got the money, he has you scared silly. I'll bet he hasn't got it now, anyway. What about that advert in the paper?'

'That was just a blind. The police could have put it in. I bet they don't know he's holding the dinaro.'

'If we got married I could go and claim it properly for you. Man and wife are one.'

'Yes, and Wife is one when she's turned Man over to the coppers, so's she can get the money.'

'You know I wouldn't shop my own husband.'

'I don't know anything of the kind. Nobody knows what anybody will do for money. I've told you I'll see you get plenty if you stand by me. That's as near as you get to marrying me.'

'Where does he live, this bloke? I could go scouting round for you, to see what's doing.'

Matt thought about that. He assumed that it was only another attempt to get to know who had the money. 'No, thanks,' he said.

The girl stared up at the ceiling. She blew smoke upward. She smiled. 'Guess who I saw this afternoon, asking after you?'

He turned and looked at her. 'Who?' he demanded, unable to conceal his fear.

'They was asking very quiet, like. Sort of secret.'

His voice rose. 'Who?'

'Norry Whitlow and Grubber Gurk. Two proper dead-legs.'

'You didn't tell them anything?'

'No. They was asking the friend I was with. I wonder what they wanted you for.'

'Trying to horn in, same as some more would like to do.'

'Is that all?'

'What else? Don't tell them anything about me.'

'I thought happen they had a notion you owed 'em something.'

'You can forget Whitlow and Gurk, and keep away from them. If they come near me they'll get a bullet apiece.'

The girl laughed silently. 'Do you know what Gurk called you?'

'Who cares?' was the sour retort. Then: 'What?'

'He said you was a double-crossing bastard, and Norry told him to shut up.'

Matt was about to reply when he heard a slight noise. He stared at the door, and heard a click as the knob moved back into place. Someone had quietly tried the door.

He sprang to his feet and moved silently to the old-fashioned dressing table. He stood there, waiting. The girl remained still, watching him.

Someone knocked at the door. Matt put a finger to his lips, then he opened a drawer of the dressing table and picked up an automatic pistol.

The doorknob rattled, and then the knock was repeated.

'Hello there,' a man called. 'Come on, open the door. I know you're in.'

In anger and distrust Matt looked at the girl. She met his gaze with wide eyes and shook her head. He thought: She's acting innocent. Moving across to her he snarled in a whisper: 'Ask who it is.'

'Who's there?' she called.

'It's me, Ned Higgs,' came the answer, not too loudly. And then: 'Open up. Nobody's going to hurt you.'

The two in the room looked at each other, one in rage and suspicion, the other, now, in uncontrolled pleasure and excitement. They both knew, or knew of, Ned Higgs. He was an important person in their eyes; Dixie Costello's lieutenant, no less, therefore almost a boss mobster himself. His business was Costello's business, obviously. It was business which did not allow for opposition in those circumstances. They both knew that the door would have to be opened for Higgs. Nevertheless, the girl called: 'What do you want?'

'I want to talk to the fellow who's with you. And I'm not going to wait all day.'

Matt made up his mind. He put the pistol in his pocket and went to the door. The girl rolled off the bed and went to the dressing table, with her fingers busy at her hair.

When the door was open, Higgs took a good look into the room before he entered. Behind him loomed a huge figure; a massive, slouching, slack-faced fellow known as the Dog.

'Hello, Mavis,' said Higgs, stepping into the room. 'I didn't know you knew this young fellow-me-lad.'

She smiled. 'It's him who knows me. I'm worth knowing.'

'I'll bet you are. But just now I don't want you here. Buzz off for a while.'

She bridled. 'I'm not going to be turned out of my own room like that!'

'Beat it. Stay out on the mat with the Dog.'

'Not me. I'm not going to be alone with that great brute.'

Higgs's expression did not change. He looked at his watch,

then he put his hand in his pocket and brought out two half-crowns.

'It's always women who make the bother, and bother I do not want just now,' he said. 'The pubs are open again. Take this dollar and go get yourself a drink.'

'That's different,' the girl said. She took the money and picked up a coat which had been folded over the iron bedrail. 'Cheerio,' she said as she slipped into the coat and departed.

Higgs said to the Dog: 'I'll whistle if I want you,' and closed the door on him. He went and leaned on the high Victorian fireplace, and looked Matt up and down.

'So you're Matt Spurr,' he said. 'How did you get to be with Mavis?'

'I knew her. I've been with her a time or two.'

'How much is she costing you?'

'I keep doling out a quid to her.'

'A quid a time isn't bad, with home comfort as well. You could do worse.'

Matt went and sat on the bed. 'You didn't come here to talk about Mavis. What are you after?'

'I've come to talk to you for your own good, over a matter of ten thousand nicker.'

Matt scowled. 'There's nothing to talk about. That money's mine.'

'If you can get it.'

'I'll get it all right.'

Higgs spoke in kindly tones. 'Not a chance, kid. You don't seem to understand the situation. You know who my boss is. Well, he's been engaged by some very big people to look after this business. These big people have just had *twenty* thousand nicker took off 'em by the police. They'd paid ten thousand to you for it, so that's thirty thousand they've lost.'

'Just a minute. It wasn't my fault they lost the twenty.'

'Some people could say it was, in a way. But we'll keep to the point. When they lost the twenty, the deal was automatically cancelled, and they want their ten thousand back.'

'Well, they're not going to get it.'

'Oh yes, they are. It's their own money, man. Their own hard-earned money. Naturally they're going to get it back. But they're going to be generous with you. You can have five hundred if you do as you're told. You're lucky. I wouldn't give you a sausage meself, after what you did.'

'After what I did?'

'Shot two of the boys. Two of my mates.'

'They were going to bash my head in, and rob me!'

'Only after you run away. That's all part of the game, sonny. It doesn't mean you have to go killing folk.'

Matt was almost weeping with frustration. 'It's all Dixie Costello's fault. If he hadn't tried to get the whole bloody lot, everything would have been all right.'

'This is no time for recriminations, as Churchill said. And you don't want to go saying things like that about Mr. Costello. You might easy get run over and lose a leg. Mr. Costello had nothing to do with it. Those boys was working on their own.'

'I don't believe it.'

'What you believe don't matter. You're the wrong man to start moralizing. You was only the bag boy on that bank job, but your mates trusted you to look after the money because they never dreamed a little twirp like you 'ud have the nerve to skedaddle with it. But you had the nerve, all right. You made a deal all on your own, and what you got out of it was going to be all yours. You don't have a leg to stand on. Anybody has as much right to that money as you.'

'Then why bother to come and talk to me about it?'

'Because it so happens you've got some sort of *legal* right to it. You can't exercise that right without surrendering to the police and admitting you had the bank's money. You can say you was just the errand lad for the others, and get off light. You'll admit trading the money in, and getting the ten thousand. That'll make it yours.'

'A lot of good it'll do me when I'm in the nick.'

'If you work the job right you might get off with as little

as two years. With remission for good conduct, that's only sixteen months.'

'I think you've forgot something, haven't you?'

'I've forgot nothing, kid. You mean the shooting. Somebody else did the shooting.'

'Who?'

'This man Eaglan, who used to be a copper.'

'*Used* to be a copper?'

'Yes. Did you think he still was one? You don't know nothing, do you kid? You'll grow up sometime, if you live that long.'

'How did he do the shooting?'

Higgs gave his explanation of how Eaglan had killed two men. Matt listened with a sour, derisive grin, but he was secretly appalled. Obviously Costello and Higgs knew exactly what had happened in Burleigh Street. Had they been talking to Eaglan? Were they in league with him? Was this a trap so skilfully hidden that he could not see it while he looked at it?

'So you see,' Higgs concluded. 'Simple, isn't it?'

'Is it? Why did Eaglan advertise the money in the paper?'

'Assuming he did do that, let the coppers worry about it. They know that all crooks do daft things at some time or other. When they've got Eaglan right, they'll soon dream up reasons for everything he did.'

'And do you think they'll believe *me*?'

'It don't matter what they believe. They've got to put your statement on record no matter what you say. And they've got to take action to find out whether it's true or not, because they know that a defending counsel someday will be asking 'em if they did that little thing, and if not, why not. And when they make their inquiries they'll find that your tale has corroboration.'

'Have you a lawyer laid on for me?'

'The coppers will ask you which solicitor you want. You'll ask for Mr. Whiteside, of Whiteside and Aspin. He'll look after you. So we're all set, except for the gun. You better let me have that.'

'You're not taking my gun. I need that for protection.'

'Are you scared Gurk and Whitlow will find you?'

'You know everything, don't you? Those two are looking for me. They'd tear me to pieces. I've got to have my gun.'

Higgs smiled. 'I've got a gun as well. See.'

Matt saw. A short-barrelled revolver had appeared in Higgs's right hand.

'We don't use guns, laddie, but we've got 'em,' said the mobster. 'Guns is silly, we always think. They make too much evidence. What sort of a gun you got?'

'A P-thirty-eight.'

'Pooh. A poor man's Luger. It jammed, didn't it? It'll jam again, I don't doubt. I brought this old six-shooter because I thought you'd want to have a gun. Take it, and give me yours.'

He proffered the revolver. Matt took it and examined it. It seemed to be in order, and it was loaded.

'It's all accounted for,' said Higgs. 'You'll leave it somewhere before you give yourself up to the bogies. But if they happen to pick you up while you're still carrying it, you'll say you bought it for a fiver outside the George and Dragon Sunday night about eight o'clock. You bought it off a lad called Pedlar Palmer. That's his nickname.'

'Yes, I know him.'

'And Pedlar knows you. He's laid on. He has a likely tale about where he got the gun, but he might have to stand a fine. That won't bother him. Somebody else will be paying it.'

Matt gave his P-38 to Higgs. Whatever happened he was better without it, now that he had another gun. 'What do I do about Whitlow and Gurk?' he asked.

'Please yourself, boy. Whatever you do, you won't make 'em want to kill you any more than they do now. If you sing a song and put 'em in the nick for ten years apiece, they won't be able to do you any harm. Not till they come out, at any rate. You got all the advantages. They're the old lags with bad records, and you're the youngster they lured into crime. You'll plead guilty and tell all you know.

"Since his arrest the prisoner Spurr has given every assistance to the police." That's what the top copper will have to say, and if he don't say it willingly your lawyer will make him. You'll get leniency. Nobody will dare mention the shooting job at the trial for the bank job. That'd be against the law.'

Matt did not reply. He was deep in thought.

'Right,' Higgs said heartily. 'So we're all set. You know what to say.'

'Aye, but I'm not sure I'm going to say it. I've got to have time to think before I hand myself over to the bobbies.'

'All right. I'll come and see you again tomorrow morning.'

'Yes, and come with a better offer than five hundred quid. That's ridiculous.'

The smile went from Higgs's face. 'I'm being very patient with you,' he said in a voice like a rasp. 'You're making with the false indignation, and all the time you're thinking to yourself that you're going to stick to the whole ten thousand, once you get it. Don't delude yourself. We aren't going to all this trouble for the sake of your blue eyes. It's a short sentence and five ones if you play along with us. If you want to play on your own, it's a quicklime grave and nothing.'

13

CONK CONQUEST'S impressive nose surfaced like the
dorsal fin of a shark as he threw his head back in an effort
to drain the last drop from a medium-sized brandy glass.
He put the glass down and looked at it with dislike. There
was still a small quantity of liquid in it.

He glanced round at the luxury of Dixie Costello's
living room. 'Are you absolutely sure the coppers don't have
this place wired for sound?' he asked.

'Absolutely is the word,' said Dixie. 'They can't get near.
Besides, it's unethical. The Chief Constable don't believe in
it. Soppy bastard.'

'So I can talk freely,' said Conk. 'And I'm saying it's the
last time anybody gets me mixed up in a job of this sort.'

'What's your moan? You're safe. You took no risk.'

The biggest nose in the North of England reared up again
as Conk looked prayerfully at the ceiling. ' "No risk," he
says. And I'm fifty hundreds out of pocket.'

'That's only temporary. You'll get it back. You're as safe
as Windsor Castle all along the line.'

'I'm not so sure about that, either. What about that
copper prying around at the gym?'

Dixie was surprised. 'Is he still there?'

'No. He knows he's rumbled. I arranged for him to take
a hiding. It didn't work. *He* dished out the hiding and
cleared off. He's quite a boy, is yon. Pity he's a bogie.'

'You can forget about him,' said Dixie confidently. 'He
knows nothing about you. He was seeking Sable Spurr.'

'He was seeking young Matt too, by all accounts. All right,
I've forgot him. But I haven't forgot my five thousand.'

'It's as good as in your pocket. It's only a matter of
waiting.'

'So you say. I can see how Matt might get the money, but you've just heard Ned say he hasn't agreed to anything yet.'

'What's agreeing got to do with it? He won't keep his word one way or the other, no matter what he agrees to. What *he* says don't matter a damn.'

'Right. So we know he's going to stick to the money if he can. How are we going to get it off him when he's safe in the nick?'

'He'll pay us off a thousand a time, under pressure. If he doesn't, I'll make his life a hell on earth. I've got influence in every gaol in England.'

Conk stared in astonishment which changed to something like admiration as his agile brain considered the possibilities of the idea. He knew that Dixie and men of his kidney in other cities formed a loose, nameless association. They had understandings with regard to territory, and occasionally they helped each other in small matters. If Dixie wanted to trace a welsher, or any other person who had 'twisted' him, he expected assistance from distant friends, as he was prepared to assist in his own 'manor'. Like Dixie himself, these powerful friends were acquainted with tough, brutal men who were in prison for their crimes. Between them, the boss mobsters had men in every prison who could be compelled or induced to do their bidding. Yes, Dixie had influence. Where he lacked it, Conk himself might have it. Matt Spurr's life in prison could be made unbearable by other prisoners, and the torture could be applied in such a way that the prison authorities would be unable to stop it. They could move Matt from place to place, but wherever he went the torturers would be waiting for him. They could even give him a new identity, but the prisoners' intelligence system would ultimately defeat them.

'That's quite an idea,' Conk admitted. 'But it's got snags. The screws'll know what's going on, even if they can't stop it. When Matt starts sending you cheques for a thousand a time, they'll tip the coppers off.'

'Grow up!' Dixie implored. 'It won't be like that at all.

If a man gets interested in finance while he's in the cooler, there's nothing to stop him investing his money, is there?'

'That's much better. He'll buy the shares he's told to buy, and they'll be worth ha'pennies and pennies.'

'You're beginning to get the idea. Spurr has been promised five ones. The shares might be worth that much altogether. I don't have any of that sort myself, but I know where I can get 'em for very little. If I can't get enough, I'll start a company or two myself.'

'Using a nominee, of course.'

'Too true. We've got to have a front. Nobody will ever be able to connect us with the job. They won't be able to touch the nominees, either.'

'I'd better start looking around for dud shares.'

'Sure. There's plenty of worked-out gold mines.'

'Copper too. So the police get Matt in the morning, whether he agrees or not?'

Dixie shook his head. 'I've been thinking about that,' he said. 'I don't see why we should wait.' He turned to Ned Higgs, who had been sitting quietly, listening. 'You left a cover on him, I suppose?'

Higgs nodded. 'Bert and Sammy. The Dog is too noticeable.'

'Are you in touch?'

Higgs looked at his watch. 'Nine o'clock,' he said. 'If I'm not at home, they'll phone me here.'

'Twenty minutes,' said Dixie. 'I'll lay six to four young Spurr is busy buying himself a good time while he still has the chance. He'll be in a pub, somewhere. So why wait till morning? If he gets picked up in a pub he'll think it's his own fault, and it don't matter if he doesn't.'

'Once we hear from Waddy, tonight should be all right,' Higgs agreed. 'Everything else is set.'

'In that case,' said Conk, reaching for a bottle, 'I'll have another drop of brandy.'

Ten minutes later the doorbell rang, and Higgs went down the stairs to let in a man whom he called Waddy. This was a short, plump, quick man who had a natural gift for repairing watches, tuning motor engines, and opening locked doors with keys of his own design. Since his last three-year sentence for shop-breaking he had opened doors only at Costello's bidding.

Dixie was glad to see him. 'Good lad,' he said. 'You managed?'

Waddy nodded. 'Easy. The back door has a lock like a barn. The bloke likes everything tidy. I found a locked drawer with his name on it. I put it at the back of the drawer, under some paper.'

'You're sure nobody saw you at all?'

'Nobody saw me.'

'You remember what I told you?'

Waddy's gaze did not waver. 'You said it was of the greatest importance that I shouldn't take a thing. I didn't touch nothing, Dixie. Not even a flashlight bulb.'

'Good. Help yourself to a drink,' said Dixie. 'We won't be long now.'

At five minutes past nine the telephone began to ring. Higgs answered it. He said 'Hello,' and 'Yes' three times, and 'Hang on there'. Then he put down the receiver.

'You were right, Dixie,' he said. 'Matt Spurr is in Jimmy Ganders, and he's not with Mavis.'

'Right. Have him picked up straight away. Who will you have for the tip-off?'

Higgs considered. 'We don't want somebody who'll take his time and maybe sleep on it,' he said. 'It'd better be one of our own lot, acting anonymous. How about Waddy here? He can talk like a female impersonator.'

'Off you go, Waddy,' said Dixie. 'Go and coo to the cops.'

.   .   .   .   .

At about eight o'clock on that Tuesday evening the troubles of Inspector Pearson began to come to an end, while the troubles of Chief Inspector Martineau merely began.

Martineau was having his first evening at home in a week, and Pearson telephoned him from Headquarters. 'Sorry to bother you,' he said. 'But the job is moving a bit. Goosey Bright has intimated that he wishes to make a statement, and he says you had better listen as well. I'm just setting off to Farways now. Shall I run round and pick you up?'

'I can read the statement tomorrow, can't I?' Martineau demanded. Then it occurred to him that there might be some question which Pearson might leave unasked. He did not like to be at the beck and call of a crook, but he could not afford to miss any information. 'All right,' he said. 'You'd better call for me.'

Goosey had been remanded in custody to Her Majesty's Prison of Granchester, commonly called Farways Gaol. On the short journey there Pearson said: 'Goosey knows we've got him right. If this statement is just an admission with no new information, I'll belt his ear-hole. But with him asking for you, somehow I feel a bit hopeful.'

'He probably just wants to ruin my evening,' Martineau growled. Pearson looked at him in surprise, and was silent thereafter.

They left the car beside the high, dark prison wall, and rang the bell of a small door of the main gate. When the gate was opened one of them said: 'Pearson, Granchester City,' and the other said: 'Martineau, same force.'

The prison officer on gate duty nodded when he heard the names. He may have recognized one or both of them, because he did not ask for credentials. 'The C.P.O.'s office,' he said. 'You know the way?'

Pearson said that he knew the way. A second door was unlocked for them and then they were in the open air again, walking on concrete towards the dark mass of the administration block. There may have been a phone call, because a second prison officer was waiting for them, and he led them to the C.P.O., a man spare and upright in his blue uniform, with a friendly smile on his thin, intelligent face.

'We get no rest, do we?' he said as he shook hands. 'Take a pew. Goosey will be here in a minute.'

It was a clean, Spartan room. They sat down on hard but not uncomfortable chairs and lit cigarettes.

'Has he said anything while he's been in?' Pearson wanted to know.

The C.P.O. shook his head. 'There's been nothing reported to me. He fancies himself a cut above most of the backward boys we have here, and he doesn't mix much. He's behaving very well, though. Paving the way for the cushy and superior job he thinks he ought to have when he comes back for the long stay.'

There was a knock on the door, and Goosey appeared between two prison officers. They brought him in, sat him down, went out and closed the door. Goosey looked at the three men who remained. He sniffed hungrily. 'I could do with a smoke, too,' he said.

Pearson had taken the seat across the desk from him. After a glance at the C.P.O., who nodded, he pushed an open packet of Senior Service and his lighter towards the prisoner. Goosey said: 'Thanks,' without gratitude, and lit a cigarette. He smoked greedily.

Pearson took out his official pocket book and laid it on the desk. Unlike Martineau, who hated to type and knew not a pothook of shorthand, he had been a police clerk at one time in his career, and he was a competent shorthand writer.

'I'm ready, Goosey,' he said briskly. 'I hope you haven't brought us out here to listen to a lot of bull.'

Goosey blinked. 'You've never heard anything but the truth from me,' he said with dignity.

'Let's say we've never heard anything, and leave it at that. I've never heard that you ever made a statement before.'

'So you're suspicious?'

'Don't let that bother you! I'm always suspicious. Let's begin at the beginning, shall we? Were you all set to take the Northern Counties Bank money before the job was done?'

'No. It was kept dead squat till it was done.'

'What was the first you heard about it?'

'I saw it in the paper, with a picture of Detective Inspector Pearson arriving at the scene of the crime.'

116

'We don't need that. What was the next thing you heard?'

'It was quite simple. The same day that I read about the job in the paper, I found to my surprise that I was being tailed. It was a young fool in a leather jacket. So I went along Lacy Street and into Maxim's store. This was about three o'clock in the afternoon and the place was fairly crowded. I stopped to look at some shoes on the ground floor and the youngster came up to me there. It was as good a place as any for us to talk; no coppers except store snoopers anywhere about. He said his name was Matt Spurr and he knew who I was. He was, he said, acting as middle-man for some jaspers who had something to sell. He was very cautious. We talked around the thing for a while, and eventually he told me what it was. I can't say I was surprised, except maybe at Spurr's inexperience. I told him I could get some used money and we came to terms. I suggested that the actual deal should be in the daytime, but he objected. He didn't want to be seen, he said. Twelve o'clock at night was safest for him. I didn't think so, but I didn't argue. We arranged for him to phone me the day after, from a public box.'

'Phone to where?' Pearson asked. 'Where were you?'

Goosey smiled. 'In another public box. The one in York Road, near the Odeon Cinema. I happen to know the number.'

'All right. Go on.'

'That's all for the first day. He phoned me as arranged, at twelve noon the day after. That was Friday the seventeenth. I set the time of the deal for midnight on Tuesday the twenty-first. He got into a lather about that. Wanted it sooner. I said no soap. A deal like that couldn't be arranged in five-and-twenty minutes. So he agreed. We arranged to talk again on the phone at ten o'clock on Tuesday night, so that I could give him the final details. I stipulated that when he came to me, he must come alone. He agreed when I said that I would be alone, too.

'That was all right, so far. I never dreamed he'd have

the money in his possession all this time, though I ought to have, when he made the fuss about delay. Not knowing where the money was, I had no idea which way he'd come to me, though I assumed he'd come most of the way in a car. So I picked on a phone box in Burleigh Street as the last place for him to report. It's just a five minutes walk from the office I'd taken as Acropolis Trading Company. I didn't know him, you see, and he seemed so green. I had to be careful.

'But everything seemed to be all right. At ten o'clock Tuesday night I talked to him, and told him to be at the Burleigh Street phone box at five to twelve, with the goods. From there I would tell him the meeting place. He was there, all right, and he wasn't as green as I had thought. He had two fellows tagging along behind, for protection no doubt. I know that because a friend of mine was watching from inside a shop across the road, sitting in the dark with a telephone at his elbow.

'I was waiting at Acropolis Trading then. My friend informed me that Spurr was at the phone box, and that two of his pals had him under remote control. That seemed to be reasonable, so long as the friends stayed at a safe distance from me. I gave the phone box a tinkle, and he answered straight away. I told him where I was, and he came. I didn't see his friends at all, so that was all right. We swapped, twenty thousand hot notes for ten thousand cool and dirty ones. I had a peep outside and everything was quiet. We shook hands and he left me. I peeped again to see if all was clear as he went away. I saw him pass by that gas-lamp across the street, at the corner of Lucy Street. It was then that I saw his friends. They came to meet him near the light, and I recognized them. Bert Kaplan and Joe Ray. There was a bit of talk, and Spurr laughed and patted his suitcase of money. Then Spurr went out of sight round the corner with the case, and the others waited a few seconds before they went in the same direction. So there you have it. That's all I can tell you.'

Pearson shot a quick, uneasy glance at Martineau, then

he said: 'I think there might be a little more. Who was going to handle the money in Belgium?'

Goosey smiled once more, and shook his head slowly as he helped himself to another cigarette. 'I can't tell you that,' he said. 'I can *never* tell you that.'

'The Antwerp police raided the address of the consignees. They found a nameplate on a door and an empty warehouse room. And nobody has been near the place at all.'

Goosey's smile grew wider. 'I'm so happy to hear that. Thanks for telling me.'

'Who was your friend who saw Spurr at the phone box in Burleigh Street?'

'Why do you want to know? Did he do something wrong?'

'It depends how much he knew.'

'He knew nothing at all. He was paid to watch that phone box, and then follow to Acropolis Trading to see that there was no funny business, and then go home.'

How did he get into the shop?'

'He persuaded the shopkeeper to lend him a key.'

'Rubbish.'

Goosey shrugged. 'He told me that he simply asked for the key, and it was given to him. He was so grateful that he left fourpence to pay for the phone call.'

'In that case he committed no offence. Who is he?'

'Barney Slatters.'

Pearson's own smile became bitter. 'So Slatters merely had to ask for the key. What would he have done if he hadn't got it? Broke the man's two arms and two legs?'

'He told me that he didn't threaten the man at all.'

'No. He wouldn't have any need. It's time we did something about him. Who put up the ten thousand?'

The sudden question did not startle Goosey. He had been expecting it for the last five minutes.

'Why, I did, of course,' he answered.

'You never had ten hundreds!'

'If you only knew. I was in business for a long time before the police were lucky enough to stumble over Summit

Supplies. I had money here and there, in quite large amounts.' Goosey sighed. 'But not much now, I'm afraid.'

'Are you trying to tell me that you alone put up the whole of the ten thousand for that crooked money deal?'

'That is exactly what I am trying to tell you. I put nearly all my eggs in one basket, I'm sorry to say. But that's the way of business. To accumulate you must speculate.'

As yet Martineau had not spoken. Now he rose to his feet. 'I don't want to listen to this lying bastard any more,' he said. 'I'm going. I'll wait outside where the air is cleaner.'

He went out. He did not see Goosey's sly grin, but Pearson saw it. 'Why did you particularly ask for Chief Inspector Martineau to be here?' he asked.

'I thought a true story might make him happy,' was the bland reply. 'I'm only too pleased to do anything I can for Martineau. Anything in the way of prussic acid or strychnine, that is.'

'That'll do from you,' said the C.P.O. 'You aren't as safe as all that.'

Pearson grinned as he closed his notebook. 'He wouldn't have dared to make that crack in front of Martineau,' he told the C.P.O. Then he turned again to Goosey. 'Did Spurr give the names of any of his mates in the bank job?' he asked, as if that were an unimportant afterthought.

'I'll try to remember,' Goosey answered.

Pearson understood him only too well. 'You'll remember when you're told to remember,' he said. 'All right, I'll send the statement tomorrow, for you to sign.' And to the C.P.O. 'Shove him back in his rat-hole.'

•   •   •   •   •

Martineau was waiting outside, staring moodily at the stars above the black silhouette of prison wall and gate tower. 'Nice news,' he growled as he and Pearson strode across the concrete. 'Goosey has been told what to say and when to say it. I can see a pattern in all this, and I'm predicting that we shall get a whisper to pick up Matt Spurr at any moment.'

14

At 9.20 p.m. a clerk at Police Headquarters received the news that Matt Spurr had been seen in the establishment known as Jimmy Ganders. The information was transmitted to him by telephone, and he knew that it was a pay telephone because he heard the informer press Button A. He asked for the informer's name, but did not get it. He was a policeman of experience, but he failed to establish the speaker's sex from the voice. He noted that it was either a masculine contralto or a feminine tenor. Then he decided that such words were not suitable for police work. He crossed out the phrase and wrote: 'Mannish woman or womanish man.' That was an error. The first description was fairly accurate, but the second was entirely wrong. There was nothing womanish about Waddy.

Detective Sergeant Devery happened to be the senior man in the C.I.D. when the information came through. Five minutes after hearing it he arrived at Jimmy Ganders in a C.I.D. car, in company with Detective Constable Cassidy. The clerk at Headquarters had broadcast his news, and an Area Patrol car with two men in uniform rolled up at the same time. 'Watch the back,' Devery said to the Traffic men. He and Cassidy went in by the front door.

Jimmy Ganders, despite its quaint name, could not be described as a typical English inn, or tavern, or hotel. It was a gin palace, and a shabby one at that. The public part of it consisted of one large uncarpeted room with a long bar, with two rows of bolted-down tables running parallel to the bar. The chairs and stools were not bolted down. They could be picked up and thrown, and their condition indicated that this occasionally happened to them. At the far end of the room, between the two doors respectively marked Ladies and Gents, was a small stage. On the stage there was an orchestra of two. There was a drummer who looked like an idiot and played like one, and there was a stout old woman who was weary, wise, and competent. The women habituées of the place were not prostitutes, they were paid amateurs. The male customers were men who sought such women, and youths who came to titter and stare.

When Devery pushed open the inner door he did not stand and gaze. He walked straight on down the room, looking around as he went. At that time on Tuesday night there were about fifty customers in the place, and the two barmen and the two burly waiters were busy. The sergeant and his companion were immediately observed, but only by a few people. There was not the apprehensive hush which usually descended on Jimmy Ganders when the police walked in. Before the silence became generally noticeable Devery was three-quarters of the way down the room, standing beside a table where a young man sat with a girl. Cassidy moved up and stood behind the man.

The couple at the table had their heads together over their drinks. They were as deeply engrossed as two people making a bargain. Devery looked at a leather jacket and a mop of dark hair which had some red in it. When he spoke, there was enough stillness in the room for him to be heard.

'Is your name Matthew Spurr?' he asked.

The young man looked up quickly. He sat back, and put his right hand inside his jacket. Behind him, Cassidy stopped that move with a flick of his wrist which nobody saw. He chopped down on the junction of shoulder and neck, not far from the spine. The young man's arm became temporarily useless. Cassidy took a firm grasp of the dark hair with his left hand, and leaned over to remove a revolver from numbed fingers. He looked at the revolver, and dropped it into his pocket. He transferred his grip to the collar of the leather jacket. Fingers as big as bananas

122

tightened on jacket and shirt as he began to lift. 'Come along, Spurr,' he said gently.

So Matt Spurr was arrested without trouble. In a company where nine out of ten hated the police, men who had half risen to go to his aid sat down when they saw the revolver. Englishmen of all types disapprove of hand guns. Guns make cowards brave. Guns turn straight fights into hanging jobs. Only mugs use guns.

Martineau and Pearson were waiting in the C.I.D. when the two detectives arrived with their prisoner. They looked at him more in appraisal than curiosity, trying to measure his qualities before the inquisition began. Martineau could not see much character in the surly young face, but he saw as much as he had expected to see.

'Have you had him in the charge room?' he asked.

'Yes sir,' Devery replied. 'The gaoler has his stuff. Nothing much.'

'Except this,' said Cassidy, taking the revolver from his pocket.

Martineau examined the weapon. It was a thirty-two. The gun used in the Burleigh Street job had been of different calibre. He made no comment.

'Take him into the grill room,' he said. 'Have a shorthand writer laid on.'

The two subordinates went away with their prisoner. Martineau held the gun in his hand. He looked at Pearson with a wry smile. 'See what I mean?'

The inspector nodded. 'Where's the other gun?'

'Oh, we shall find it,' said Martineau. 'I haven't the slightest doubt about that.'

They went along to the windowless, soundproof Interrogation Room where – much to their regret – the only Third Degree they could practise was oral and psychological. They found Spurr seated at a central table under a strong light. Martineau took a chair opposite him, and Pearson sat a little to one side. Devery and Cassidy sat with their backs to the wall near the door, and the shorthand writer sat at a small table in the corner.

Martineau looked at the prisoner for some time, and then he said: 'You had a hell of a nerve. What made you go to a place like Jimmy Ganders?'

The answer was given without hesitation: 'I thought I'd have a final fling. I was going to give myself up in the morning.'

'By arrangement?'

'I don't know what you mean. I was going to give myself up.'

'Who told you to do that?'

'Nobody.'

'What made you come to that decision?'

'I found out something. I thought Cliff Eaglan was a detective, and I was scared he'd be in league with some more cops. I thought they had framed me.'

'For what?'

'You know what. Then I found out Eaglan wasn't a cop, and that made it a bit different. I decided to give myself up.'

'So you got rid of the murder gun first. Is that it?'

'I didn't get rid of any gun. You've got my gun.'

Martineau took the revolver from his pocket. 'This? Where did you get it?'

'Do I have to tell?'

'No, but you will. Go on, spill it.'

'I want to get everything off my chest. I know I've been a fool, but I want to do the best I can now.'

'Very touching. Go on, then. Do the best you can.'

'I got the gun off a lad called Pedlar Palmer, last Sunday night. I gave him a fiver for it. It was outside the George and Dragon, about eight o'clock.'

'What did you do with the gun you had last Tuesday night?'

'I didn't have a gun then. That revolver is the first gun I ever had.'

'Why did you need a gun?'

'For protection. There's two men I'm scared of.'

'Two men who were with you in the Northern Counties Bank job?'

'The two men who *did* the job. I was only the go-between with the money.'

'Who did the job?'

'Norry Whitlow and Grubber Gurk.'

'Nobody else?'

'Nobody else that I know of.'

Carefully, as if he did not wish to be heard, Pearson got up from his chair and began to move towards the door. Martineau watched the movement out of the corners of his eyes. 'Clearing up nicely,' he observed. He might have been commenting on the weather, but for the sarcasm in his voice. Pearson's answer was a somewhat shamefaced grin. His own case was sailing along like a dreamboat, while Martineau's was being shot to pieces. He closed the door very quietly as he went out.

'All right,' said Martineau to the prisoner. 'Tell it from the beginning. Start with Whitlow and Gurk.'

'Well, I'd known them a while, but not very well. Then they suddenly started to get right friendly. I used to have a drink or two with 'em. Then one day Whitlow said he knew a bank where he could get in. He said it was a two-man job, for him and Gurk, but they needed somebody they could trust, to hold the take for them after the job. That was because they both had records and they were afraid the police would turn 'em up. They offered me a ten per cent cut for looking after the take and not touching it till they gave the word. Well, I was down to the price of a pint, so I let 'em talk me into it. Sunday afternoon was the time they picked to start the job, because they could work in a closed yard at the back of the bank. The idea was to start in daylight just so it would be dark when they finished. They got a car – I don't know where – and picked me up Sunday at three. They parked the car behind Lacy Street, in that back street off Higgitt's Passage. I stayed with the car while they did the job.'

'Hold it,' said Martineau. 'Now you're deviating. You didn't stay with any car. Start that bit again.'

'Well, I *intended* to stay with the car, but they asked me to go with 'em and be the lookout, so I did.'

'That's better. They wanted you right in it, with them. Go on.'

'Yes, I suppose I was in, but I didn't bust any safes. I'll give it to you straight now. Norry drove the car round to the back of the bank. Grubber was the peterman, and he climbed over the wall into the yard. He did it with a rope and a grapple. Then I got on the wall and Norry handed Grubber's stuff up to me, and I handed it down to Grubber. Then I unhooked the grapple and Norry took it away with him while he parked the car where I said. Then he came back and used the grapple to come over the wall to us. While we waited for him Grubber started getting into the bank. There was no door in the yard, and all the windows had bars. Grubber used a thing like a jack to prise two bars far enough apart for him to get through, then he jemmied the window and he was in. Norry passed him his stuff and went in after him. I didn't see 'em again for six hours.'

'You sat on the window sill in the yard. You left your cigarette ends.'

'That's right. I didn't go into the bank at all. All the windows opposite, looking down into the yard, belonged to offices in Walsh Street. It was my job to watch the windows and give the alarm if I saw anybody looking my way. I never saw anybody at all: there was nobody in the offices. All the same, I felt a lot better when it came dark. I didn't light any cigarettes in the dark.'

'Did you hear them blow the safe?'

'Yes, but only just. They did a good job of muffling it. They came out soon after that, with just the one case. I thought that was Grubber's tackle, but they said it was the money: they'd left the tackle behind. Then Norry went over the wall and we waited till he came back with the car. They took me home and I sneaked the case up to my room, and that was it.'

'Did you know it was new money before you looked at it?'

'Yes. There were two safes in the vault, and Grubber picked the wrong one. There was nothing but new money in it. When he'd blown it he said he was so tired his hands were trembling and clumsy, so he didn't try the other one. Norry knew I was hard up, so he gave me some spending money so I wouldn't be tempted to spend any of the new stuff.'

'Did you see them after that?'

'Yes. Every day for a week or more, up to the Tuesday when I did the swop with Goosey Bright. I didn't drink with 'em. Just gave 'em the nod that everything was all right.'

'How did you contact Goosey?'

'I heard two fellows talking in the Casino Club. One of 'em pointed him out to the other. I'd heard of him, and I started to get ideas straight away. Ten per cent didn't seem to be much of a cut. I thought if I flogged the lot I could open a bank account with the money, then clear off to South Africa and have it transferred to me there. So when Goosey went out I followed him. I spoke to him in Maxim's, and we made a deal, one used note for two new ones.'

Matt went on to give the details of the deal in stolen money. Martineau had learned of them before, from Goosey. So far, he had been hearing the truth. Henceforward he expected to hear something different.

'Why did you choose to do it at midnight?' he asked.

'I didn't fancy doing it when people were about. I didn't know just how closely Norry and Grubber were watching me. The only thing wrong with midnight was that I had to have protection. So I went to two pals of mine, Bert Kaplan and Joe Ray. I offered 'em a tenner apiece to do escort duty. I said I was going to flog a suitcase full of Havana cigars that I'd pinched. Their job was to follow on behind me, and if a stray copper stopped me and asked about the suitcase, one of 'em was going to break a shop window straight away, and have the copper chasing him. They jumped at the chance of an easy tenner.

'I met Goosey at a place called the Acropolis something or other, and we did the deal. Everything went perfect till I was walking back along Burleigh Street, and this Eaglan, who I thought was a copper, stepped out of a doorway. He had a gun in his hand, and a very nasty grin on his face. He said: 'I'll take that,' and pointed to the case. I was scared green. All kinds of ideas were running through my head. When coppers start taking money with guns it looks as if there's a middling deep plot somewhere. He stuck the gun in my belly as he lifted the case out of my hand, and I just couldn't move, I tell you. Then Bert and Joe came running up and he turned on them. I moved all right, then. I ran for my life. I heard some shots. I don't know how many 'cause I didn't count 'em. I ran a long way before I looked back. I saw two men on the ground, not moving, and Eaglan standing with the suitcase. He seemed to be looking in my direction. I kept on running, and I didn't stop till I was safe home.'

Martineau looked bored. But he said: 'Very good. A product of the master mind. Can you tell me why Kaplan and Ray got themselves killed over what they would assume to be an empty suitcase. You were supposed to have got rid of your imaginary cigars, weren't you?'

'Oh, I forgot to tell you about that. When I came out of the Acropolis place I spoke to them. I said: "The dirty rotter paid me out with some silver that's been huffed from somewhere, but it'll spend just the same." Bert and Joe thought there was sixty quid in silver coin in the case.'

'Didn't they think that twenty pounds in escort money was a lot to pay out of a sixty-pound deal?'

'They might have thought so, but they didn't say so. In any case they'd put it down to me being windy and flush with money at the same time.'

'So you went home. What then?'

'I didn't sleep a wink. I lay in bed sweating, and thinking about Bert and Joe, and Eaglan. I thought if there'd been a murder, or two murders, Eaglan and his pals would cook up a lot of evidence against me. Then I thought if Eaglan was keeping the money I might be able to get it back. I thought a lot about that, and the day after I told my sister a tale, and she went looking for the suitcase in his room. It was a forlorn hope, as they say. Anyway, Eaglan caught her there, and she had to make a getaway. That put me right down in the dumps. It came teatime, and we got our *Evening Guardian*. I read about the bodies found in Burleigh Street, then I looked at the Found Property column. I didn't think there'd be anything there, but I looked just the same. I saw the advert about the ten thousand quid, and I thought: "My name's McCoy". The coppers would be after me to pin a murder on me, and Norry and Grubber would be around to see if their money was safe. I walked straight out of the house and went to Mavis Reeder, a girl I know. She was the only person I could think of. I stayed with her until tonight.'

'And that's the end of *your* story.'

'I suppose it is. Who shopped me?'

'I don't know, and I wouldn't tell you if I did.'

'Will I be able to claim the money?'

'You'll have to ask somebody else.'

'I shall claim it.'

'I'm sure you will. That's the idea, isn't it? Who are you sharing it with?'

'Nobody. It's mine.'

'Has somebody been telling you the law of it?'

'No. I worked it out myself.'

'How did you find out that Eaglan was no longer a policeman?'

'Somebody told me.'

'Who?'

'I'd rather not say. There's enough people been drawn into this already.'

'It was no offence to tell you about Eaglan. The person who told you won't be drawn into it by that. Who told you?'

'I can't remember.'

'You've done all right for Whitlow and Gurk and Goosey and Pedlar Palmer. You've sung a lovely tune about them. But now you've suddenly got a conscience about somebody who did nothing wrong in giving you a bit of information. That's not so good, is it? Is it somebody you're afraid of?'

'No. I'm only afraid of Norry and Grubber.'

'Did your informant tell you that he didn't want his name to be mentioned?'

'I don't remember.'

'Was it Dixie Costello?'

'No. I don't know him.'

'Was it Ned Higgs?'

'No. Who's Ned Higgs?'

'Was it any of the Costello mob?'

'I don't know the Costello mob.'

'Did you know that Kaplan and Ray were Costello's boys?'

'No. Were they?'

Martineau suddenly leaned back in his chair. 'Take him away and lock him up,' he growled. 'I'll talk to him later.'

Devery and Cassidy took the prisoner away. The short-hand writer went away. Martineau sat alone, brooding. He was still there when Devery returned. Sensing his mood, the sergeant waited, not venturing any remark.

Eventually a wry grin appeared on Martineau's face, and he said: 'Do you think it's ever happened on God's rolling earth? Do you think it's even possible for four lying crooks like Goosey Bright, Barney Slatters, Pedlar Palmer and Matt Spurr all to be telling the truth at the same time, about the same thing?'

'No sir,' said Devery. 'I don't.'

'Not possible. Nevertheless, we must act upon the information we have received. See to it. I want Cliff Eaglan to be brought here for interrogation. Search warrants and search of his lodgings and place of work, and any other likely place. Statements from Slatters and Palmer, and appropriate action.'

'Yessir,' said Devery, turning away at once.

Martineau sat and thought about motives. He wondered how a man called Costello hoped to benefit by substituting Cliff Eaglan for Matt Spurr as a murder suspect. The main aim, he presumed, was to keep Spurr in the clear. But Spurr would go to prison for his part in a bank robbery.

While he was in prison, how could Costello take ten thousand pounds away from him? Even if he had promised to hand over the money once he was clear of the murder charge, the position was still the same. Spurr's promises were worthless, and Costello would be well aware of that. Spurr could defeat him. When he had served his sentence, he could claim police protection until he and his money were safely out of the country. Knowing the situation, the police would be compelled to give that protection to prevent the commission of a major crime.

'All right, Mister Costello,' he mused. 'It may be you'll stick your neck out too far this time.'

He hoped so. He sincerely hoped so, but he could not yet see how it might happen.

15

WHEN officers went for Cliff Eaglan they found that he was not in his lodgings. His landlady did not know where he had gone, so a general search for him was ordered. While he waited for the man to be located, Martineau went along to see what progress Pearson was making.

He found the detective inspector fairly glowing with triumph. Gurk and Whitlow were already in the cells, both men having been taken from the first public house in which they were sought, by C.I.D. men who knew them well. All their clothes had been brought from their homes to Headquarters, and the homes themselves were still being searched.

Whitlow's clothes were piled on a desk in the main C.I.D. office, under the care of a detective. Gurk's clothes were on Pearson's own desk, and when Martineau went in to see him he was examining the sole of a shoe under a strong light. Tiny particles of some metallic substance were embedded in the leather. Under the light they glittered like gold dust.

Martineau knew that Gurk and Whitlow had used an electric drill, with the bank's own power, to drill out the lock of a bronze door leading to the bank vault. Later they had drilled holes in the hard steel of the safe door, which holes they had packed with detonators and Unifrax. The particles of steel from the safe were probably too small for Pearson to identify even with a strong glass, but the workers at the police forensic laboratory would find them easily enough.

Pearson held up the shoe for Martineau to see the sparkle of the bronze particles. Martineau nodded. 'Spurr says the cigarette ends in the bank yard were his,' he remarked.

'Good, good,' said Pearson. 'If he'll give us a sample of his saliva, maybe we'll have got *him* right, too.'

'He's your least worry. Haven't you talked to the others at all?'

'No. Let 'em stew a bit. I'm betting I'll find Unifrax on their clothes and Insula in their turn-ups. When I've got that, and their shoes, I don't care what they say, or what they don't say.'

'It'll be a hundred per cent job. All property recovered. The Chief will be pleased with you.'

'And you. He knows who nailed Goosey. I'm grateful for that, you know. I must say I've had the right sort of luck with this one. How about you? Did Spurr's tale work out as you expected?'

'Oh sure. I'm up a gum tree. I've got a cast-iron case against the wrong man. In about ten minutes somebody will walk in here with the murder gun, found on premises to which Cliff Eaglan had easy access. I'll lay ten to one.'

'No takers. You'll crack it, all right. Somebody will blunder.'

'Yes. It might be me.'

'Are you absolutely sure it couldn't be Eaglan?'

'No. How can I be? There's just one chance in a million that that bunch of lovelies happens to be telling the truth. I wouldn't put the odds lower than that.'

'Will you lock Eaglan up?'

'I don't know yet. With all that evidence I shall have to do something, and that's a fact. I don't want to have to charge him with murder, but I can't let him walk about free. I'll have to see how things go.'

'Well, anything I can do, just say the word,' said Pearson, and he sounded as if he meant it.

Martineau left him then, and went to his own office. He sat down to wait, but he had no sooner put his feet on the desk than a bustle outside his door made him remove them. There was a knock, and then Cliff Eaglan was ushered into the room by Detective Constables Ducklin and Cook. Eaglan's white, worried look and Ducklin's suppressed but none the less palpable air of triumph made Martineau think that there had been a happening which would add to his difficulties.

He was not mistaken. 'Hello, Eaglan,' he said. And to Ducklin: 'Where did you find him?'

The answer was prompt. 'On enclosed premises, sir.'

Eaglan swore unhappily. 'Just the sort of crack you'd expect from Ducklin,' he growled.

Martineau held up his hand. 'Just a moment, Eaglan. Go on, Ducklin.'

Ducklin was ready and willing to go on. 'Cook and I had to wait for a warrant, then we went to search Isaacson's shop. When we got there we saw a light on the premises. When we reached the front door we caught this man emerging.'

'I work there, you fool,' said Eaglan wearily. 'I have a key.'

But Martineau held up his hand again. Obviously Ducklin had more to say.

The C.I.D. man continued. 'We brought him to Headquarters in the car. I sat with him on the rear seat. I detected a furtive movement, and caught him trying to push this down the back of the seat.'

'This' was an automatic pistol, which Ducklin had taken from his pocket. He stepped forward and put it on the desk in front of Martineau. The chief inspector did not touch it. He looked at Eaglan. 'Sit down,' he said, pointing to a chair, 'and explain.'

Eaglan met the level glance, but he looked harassed and desperate. 'I can't explain it all,' he said with a slight shake of his head. 'I've been out for a drink or two. On the way home I called at the shop for my collection book. Most of our hire-purchase customers pay their instalments at the shop, but with a few of them you've got to collect the money to stop them from getting hopelessly into arrears. I'm responsible for those. I usually collect on Fridays and Saturdays, but I also have a few calls on Tuesdays. I bring my book up to date just before closing time as a rule, but tonight we had a rush of business at the last minute, and I had to help in the shop. I meant to put the book in my pocket and enter it up at home, but I forgot. I don't like to start a day's work by finishing yesterday's, so tonight I called to make up the book. When I opened my drawer, which was locked when I left it, I got the feeling that some-body had been moving my stuff about. The drawer wasn't quite the same as when I left it. I pulled the drawer right out, and found that gun. Naturally I knew it was a plant. I slipped it into my pocket and got out of there quick. Ducklin and Cook met me at the door. I was caught with it in my pocket.'

'What were you going to do with it?'

'I hadn't had time to decide. A bit of a coincidence, isn't it, these two meeting me at the door? It almost makes me think they were lying in wait for me.'

'You think it's a police plant?'

'It looks like it. But I'll admit there never was any of that sort of caper when I was in the C.I.D.'

'How could Ducklin and Cook have been lying in wait? They had no idea you would call at the shop.'

'They could have been following me.'

'No. The word was out for you. They went to the shop to search, but they found you instead.'

'Why did you want me?'

'We've got Matt Spurr. His tale doesn't tally with yours.'

Eaglan laughed shortly. 'Did you expect it to?'

'Up to a point,' said Martineau. He opened a drawer, and took out his file on the Kaplan and Ray homicides. He opened the file. 'Would you like to tell me again exactly what happened in Burleigh Street?' he asked.

Eaglan sighed. 'Gosh, I'm tired,' he said. But he told his story again, carefully and succinctly. Martineau read the file as he listened, checking the second statement with the first. The two versions were alike, except for slight differences in phrasing.

He made no comment about this. When Eaglan had finished he closed the file and said: 'Spurr's story is that

Kaplan and Ray were with him all the time, till you shot them and stole the money.'

Eaglan drew in his breath sharply. He was silent for a short while, then he said: 'So it's my word against his'.

'He's got two witnesses to back him part of the way. You don't have any.'

Eaglan, the ex-policeman, needed only a short time to consider his position, and see it as a disinterested person would see it. 'So there are witnesses against me, and you found me with a gun – probably *the* gun – in my pocket. So be it. There's nothing I can do except keep on telling the truth. Any witness who says I'm a liar is a liar himself. I'll stick to the truth and what's more I'll stick to the money. To hell with Matt Spurr. He won't get that money if I can help it.'

Martineau nodded. He looked at his watch. 'Have you had your supper?' he asked.

'No. I'm hungry, too.'

'All right. Go out and have some fish and chips, or something. By the time you've had that, the other statements should be in. You can come back here and we'll find a nice little cell for you.'

Eaglan showed surprise, Cook grinned, and Ducklin seemed to be dumbfounded. Then Eaglan rose from his chair and departed without a word. Martineau looked at the other two. He made two fingers of each hand walk across the desk.

'I don't think he'll try to skip,' he said. 'But you fellows had better tag along and make sure.'

· · · · ·

Bill Hearn went into court the following morning, to have a look at the characters who were due to appear before the Stipendiary Magistrate. As he had expected, Sable Spurr and Nipper were in the crowded public gallery. Also present, in a group, were Eddie Ellam and some of the boys who used Blascoe's Gymnasium. Bill stared steadily at Sable until he caught her eye. She looked at him just long enough to make it understood that she despised him. He had expected something of the kind, nevertheless he was disappointed. Much too optimistically he had hoped that she would be intelligent enough to realize that his undercover job at the gymnasium had been the sort of task which any policeman might have been called upon to do. She had been so much in his mind recently that the slightness of her acquaintance with him was completely overlooked. It never occurred to him that Sable might not have thought about him at all.

Case Number One was Clifford Eaglan, on charges of highway robbery and murder. No evidence was offered. Chief Superintendent Clay asked for a remand in custody of three days, for further police inquiries to be made. The application was granted, and Eaglan was taken back to the cells.

Case Number Two was Benedict Gurk, Matthew Spurr, and Norris Whitlow. These men filed into the dock with four policemen to guard them, and the biggest of the policemen stationed himself between Matt and the other two prisoners. Bill looked curiously at Matt. He recognized him. That was the lad he had chased away from Blascoe's Gym. He studied the other two. Both of them were a little above medium height, decently and unobtrusively dressed, and between thirty and thirty-five years of age. But they were totally dissimilar in appearance. Gurk was heavily built, and obviously very strong. He had a flat, brutal face with thick, shapeless lips, very small blue eyes, and coarse, rusty-looking hair. Whitlow was dark and handsome, with a small moustache. He looked compact and quick. Bill thought that he would be the more dangerous of the two, but both men had murder in their eyes when they looked at Spurr.

In this case also no evidence was offered. There was another application for a remand in custody for three days, and it was granted. The three prisoners stood down.

Case Number Three was William Walter Bright, and now witnesses were ready to go into the box. The case against

137

Bright was complete. Depositions would be taken, and Bright would be remanded for trial at Assize. That was a certainty. Bill looked at Sable, and saw that she and Nipper were leaving the courtroom. Matt had been taken below, but he would be required as a witness in the Bright case. Bill guessed that Sable and Nipper would be allowed to see him before he returned to enter the witness box. He slipped out of court and went through the building to the entrance of the cell corridor.

He was hanging about the inner hallway there, keeping out of sight, when Matt and Sable met. He could not hear what was said, and did not want to hear. He saw Nipper standing near and looking more properly serious than miserable. Sable was the apple of Nipper's eye, not Matt. Bill could almost read his thoughts. He was standing by the boy, who had asked for what he was getting, and who had been warned by his grandfather time and time again to choose better company.

Brother and sister did not embrace, and there were no tears. Matt looked surly, though Sable did not seem to be reproving him. Bill made a guess. The sister, stronger and more able, had always spoiled the brother though she was not more than a year older than he.

After a few minutes of conversation, Matt was taken on his journey back to the courtroom by way of the cells. Sable and her grandfather turned to leave the building. As they did so, Bill walked into plain sight of them. When she saw him, Sable held her head high. She would have passed without speaking. Bill spoke.

'Do you remember me, Miss Spurr?' he asked.

'I think so,' she answered coldly. 'You're the police spy, aren't you?'

'Don't be like that,' he said. 'I didn't turn your brother in.'

'You were after him.'

'Only like any other policeman.'

'*Not* like any other policeman. You were spying on my grandfather.'

138

'It would have been me or somebody else. I was picked for the job because I could box a bit.'

'You're a fool for bein' a copper. You could make a fortune with your mitts,' said Nipper severely.

Bill looked at the old man, and realized that negotiations could be continued through him. 'You wouldn't have me in the gym, now,' he said.

Nipper could not hold a grudge for long. 'You could come all right,' he said judiciously, 'if you came in the open and said you were on the force. I've had plenty of coppers in Blascoe's in my time. There's nothin' wrong with a cop if he's honest about it.'

Bill heard the last remark, but he was looking at the girl again. He felt as if he could have spent his life looking at her.

She was aware of his glance. It melted the ice in her. Embarrassed and yet strangely thrilled, she took refuge in derision. She said: 'I'll bet he was a fine sight, running about the streets in trunks and boxing gloves.'

'Ah, but he soon bust that door down when he came back,' said Nipper, almost with pride. 'It didn't stop him a minute.'

'Oh, you!' said his grandchild, and she began to move away. He followed.

'Happen I'll see you at the gym, then,' Bill called after him.

'Happen so,' the old man replied. 'I'll have a word with Mr. Conquest about you.'

Bill was not dissatisfied with the interview. He was on speaking terms with Nipper again and, after a fashion, he had scraped acquaintance with Sable.

He returned to the C.I.D., and was informed that Martineau wanted him. He went to the chief inspector's office, knocked, and entered.

'I just saw you talking to Nipper and Sable Spurr,' he said. 'How do you stand with them?'

'Better than I did,' Bill replied. 'But not too good at that.'

'Do you think either of them would talk to you more than they would to me?'

139

'I doubt it, sir. Neither of them would trust me very far, yet.'

'Mmmm. There's something I want to find out, and I need it badly. I want to know if Nipper or Sable, or both, ever saw Matt with an automatic pistol. They may not have done. If they did, they'll be reluctant to talk about it. I've got a squad of men out around the pubs and coffee bars asking the same question, but I want the answer from Nipper or the girl if I can get it.'

'Is either of them likely to tell me that, sir?'

'No. But you never know your luck. Go and see Nipper this afternoon, and get everything he'll tell you about Matt: childhood, schooldays, ailments, jobs, the lot. Choose your time to ask him about the pistol, but don't trick him into anything. Make sure he knows what he's talking about before he answers. We don't want any lawyers saying we kidded him to come copper on his grandson.'

'Very good, sir. What about Sable?'

'You and I will go together to see her, this evening. I'll have to give her the whole picture, and then see if her conscience will work for us. Ours is a hell of a job, isn't it? We're going to try and get a girl to give evidence against her own brother. We've got to do it. Truth is where you find it.'

'I don't know Miss Spurr very well, but I think she'll be truthful.'

'Yes. And that puts her in a hell of a position if she knows anything,' said Martineau. He opened a drawer of his desk and took out a pistol. 'This appears to be called a P-thirty-eight. It's the first one I've seen. Have a look at it.'

Bill took the pistol and examined it, and handed it back.

'Would you know it again?' Martineau asked.

'Sure. Somebody who had this fancied himself as a killer. There are four notches cut along the top of the hand grip.'

'A German N.C.O. probably, during the war. All right, take it round to the laboratory; they're waiting for it. See Nipper this afternoon and get his statement, and wait for me here at six o'clock tonight.'

Bill went to the laboratory, and spent an edifying half-hour watching a ballistics expert compare bullets and cartridge cases to make sure that the P.38 was indeed the pistol which had been used in the Burleigh Street affray.

That afternoon he went to Blascoe's Gymnasium. Two o'clock was the time he chose, because it followed too closely on the lunch hour for the place to be busy. As he had expected, the big room was deserted. He looked into the office, and saw Nipper and Conk Conquest. Conk was putting silver and copper into paper money-bags, and Nipper was watching him. The old man seemed to be startled and annoyed when he looked up at Bill, perhaps because he thought that the young policeman was taking too prompt an advantage of his fair words of the morning, or perhaps of Conk's presence.

'This office is private,' he snapped. 'We're busy.'

'Oh, sorry,' said Bill, retreating a few inches.

Conk gave him a quick, sly glance. 'No sweater today, eh?' he said. And to Nipper: 'Isn't this the lad who's on the force?'

The reply was a surly affirmative. Conk addressed himself to Bill again: 'Take my advice, boy, and *stay* on the force. However good you think you are, don't let any broken-down old pugs like this one persuade you that you can make a fortune in the ring. You stick to your job.'

Bill grinned. 'I'll do that.'

'Good. So you don't need to hang around this place any more, do you?'

The snub did not take the grin from Bill's face. 'I do today,' he said. 'I'm here on duty.'

'Oh. Who are you going to try to lock up this time?'

'Nobody. I'm here to interview Nipper. I'm going to listen to him telling me what a good boy Matt has been all his life.'

'You want more evidence?'

'Evidence of character, mainly. I'll put down all he says and nothing he doesn't say.'

'Suppose I say nowt at all?' Nipper wanted to know.

141

'Surely you won't miss a chance of putting in a good word for your grandson?' Bill countered.

Conk was putting the bags of money into a brief case. 'Talk to him, Nipper,' he said. 'Say everything you can that'll help young Matt to get a lighter sentence.'

He closed the brief case and bustled out of the gymnasium. Bill stayed to question Nipper and write down his replies scrupulously. Some of the facts he noted were already known to him, that Matt's father had been killed in the war, and that his mother had since died of cancer.

'Sable were only fourteen when her mother died, an' it were a big shock to her,' he declared. 'But she set to like a little good 'un an' kept the home goin'. She were a champion little housewife, an' all. Things were a bit thin at first, but as soon as Sable could leave school she got herself a job in a grocer's shop, but she went to night school an' learned this here shorthand an' typewritin', an' got herself a daddy of a job. She's all right, is our Sable.'

'What about Matt? How did he shape?'

'Well, he were broke up at losin' his mother, too. Be sure you put that down, father died fightin' for his country an' mother died when he were a youngster. He tried his hand at various jobs, but he were a bit unlucky, like. Couldn't settle. Labourin' jobs, put. Course he knew he'd be goin' into the Army when he were eighteen, an' that didn't settle him any. Military record good, put.'

'We'll get that from the War Office.'

'Oh aye. Well, it'll be all right. He got to be a lance jack. He's a good lad when there's somebody who can rule him. We wouldn't have had this trouble if his father had been alive. Our Harry were a buckstick. He'd a-ruled him, all right.'

'What sort of job did Matt get when he came out of the Army?'

'Workin' in a warehouse. Packin' an' that. He changed three or four times, but he weren't much out of work. He's been out of work this last week or two, though. Had a row with a foreman, or summat. This foreman were pickin' on him a bit.'

'Who's your doctor?'

'O'Brien, in Glossop Road. But we never see him. None of us ever ails aught. Sable an' Matt has never had anythin' worse nor 'flu' in their lives.'

'Was Matt ever in trouble with the police as a child?'

'No. Put that. No police record at all.'

'Right. Now I'm going to ask you something rather different. I was instructed to give you due warning so that you wouldn't feel you'd been tricked into answering. Fair enough?'

Nipper's gaze was steady. 'Fair enough,' he said.

'Have you ever seen Matt with a gun? A pistol or a revolver?'

The pale old eyes flickered, but the answer came in firm tones. 'No, I never have.'

Bill nodded. He wrote down the answer and closed his notebook. He would have liked to ask if Sable was at her place of work that afternoon. He could imagine Nipper picking up the telephone and giving her details of the interview. He reflected that Martineau must have foreseen that something of the sort could happen. If Martineau did not mind, neither did he.

He had made his notes in the form of a statement. He give this to Nipper to read. The old man read, his lips moving slightly, then he signed without demur. Bill left him then, and went to Headquarters to have typed copies of the statement made. He wanted to have them ready for Martineau at six o'clock. But all the typists in the C.I.D. were too busy to bother with him. He found a typewriter which was not in use and began to make the copies himself. He had never done any typing before. He prodded away with two fingers for the rest of the afternoon and wasted a considerable amount of official stationery. But he succeeded in producing four fair copies.

16

WHEN Martineau knocked at the door of number 30 Rochester Street at a quarter past six that evening, the door was opened by Sable Spurr. She showed no surprise when she saw him. 'Hello, Mr. Martineau. Come in,' she said. She ignored Bill Hearn, and by doing so brought a faint, amused smile to the chief inspector's face. Nobody saw the smile. The girl had stepped back to make way for the visitors, and she was taking a quick glance at her reflection in the hallstand mirror. Bill had eyes only for her.

As the two men went through to the living room she took their hats. At least she took Martineau's. She tried to take Bill's without looking at him or the hat, and dropped it. Bill said: 'Sorry,' and stooped to get the hat. Flustered, Sable also stooped. The two young heads collided, but not forcibly. Blushing with embarrassment, Sable turned away and left Bill to put his own hat on the hallstand. Martineau's secret amusement grew.

'Sorry to trouble you again,' he said, when they were seated in the comfortable, homely living room. 'I have to ask you a question. This young man asked your grandfather the same question this afternoon. Did he ring you up and tell you about it?'

'No,' said Sable. 'He couldn't reach me. I've been at home all afternoon.'

'Mmmm. Well, it's a serious question, and I want you to think about it before you answer. Have you ever seen Matt with a gun? An automatic pistol.'

'No,' the girl answered promptly and firmly. 'I've never seen him with a pistol, and I've never seen a pistol in this house.'

'Well, that's definite enough. He tells me a different story to the one he told you, of course.'

'But why are you asking if Matt had a gun? Didn't Eaglan kill those two men?'

'He's been charged with the crime, mainly on the strength of Matt's statement. That statement may not be true, you know.'

Sable's eyes were troubled. 'You don't think Eaglan did it?'

'I can't say. I'm trying to get at the facts.'

'What did Grandad say about the gun?'

'More or less the same as you.'

'So we can't help you. What does Matt say now?'

Martineau told her Matt's story, and Eaglan's. When he had finished, she sat in thought.

'It would be awful if another man were punished for what Matt did,' she said at last. 'But I don't see how that can happen. Surely those other men aren't all telling lies? The man you call Goosey. What can he gain by lying about Matt and those two who were shot?'

'We have ideas about that, but we can't be certain.'

'Could I see Matt tomorrow, and talk to him in private?'

'Certainly,' said Martineau, 'I'll leave word about that. Come to Headquarters any time it's convenient for you.'

There was some further talk, mainly in verification of the general information which Bill had obtained from Nipper. Then Martineau turned to Bill. 'Can you think of anything else?' he asked.

Bill shook his head. 'No, sir.'

Martineau stood up. He smiled at Sable. 'My young colleague is a very worthy fellow,' he said. 'I gave him a rather distasteful assignment recently. Playing the spy. He had to do it because I told him to. It isn't likely that he'll ever have to do that kind of work again. He'll be too well known.'

'Why are you telling me that?' she asked.

Martineau seemed to be surprised by her tone. 'No reason really,' he said airily. 'Just idle gossip.'

145

The two policemen departed then, with Sable still ignoring Bill. But there was something in her manner which made the young man feel that there was still some chance of further acquaintance. On the way back to Headquarters he said to Martineau: 'Thanks for the good word'.

The chief inspector raised his eyebrows. 'When was that? Did I say something?'

When he was back in his own office Martineau sent for Norry Whitlow. The prisoner came with an air of willingness, and immediately asked for a cigarette. 'If you're going to ask questions I may as well get a smoke out of the job,' he said. 'What do you want? You're not on my case.'

Martineau gave him a cigarette. 'You know the case I'm on,' he said. 'Have you ever seen Matt Spurr with a firearm?'

Whitlow's eyes glinted. 'What sort of a firearm?'

'Any sort.'

'Sure. Spurr had a gun. I don't know what make, though.'

'Did you *see* the gun?'

'Of course I saw it.'

'Was it a revolver or an automatic?'

'I didn't notice. A revolver, I think.'

'You're lying, aren't you?'

Whitlow grinned. 'Yes, inspector. I'd chance my arm on a perjury rap if there was any hope of getting that little rat into trouble.'

'Then you've never seen him with a gun?'

'No. I can't say I have.'

'Take him away,' said Martineau.

'Just a minute, Inspector. You're in charge of that shooting job. Is it true Spurr gets that ten thousand quid?'

'Nobody knows, yet.'

'Well, what do you think?'

'I think *you* don't have a hope in hell of getting any of it, if that's what you want to know. Take him away, and bring Gurk!'

Gurk arrived in a surly mood, his little eyes glinting

with suspicion. He looked around carefully before he sat down, as if he feared that the room might be wired for sound. He asked for a cigarette and accepted one without thanks, and waited. Martineau asked him if he had seen Matt Spurr with a firearm. He pondered briefly, then boldly took the plunge. 'Yes, the little tea-leaf had a gun,' he said.

'What sort of a gun?'

'A revolver,' was the prompt answer. 'It looked like a thirty-eight.'

'Are you sure it wasn't an automatic?'

There was a pause. Gurk decided to stick to his tale. 'It was a revolver.'

Martineau sighed. 'You guessed wrong,' he said.

'That's a pity,' Gurk said quite seriously.

'All right. That's all I wanted to ask you.'

'But it isn't all I want to ask *you*. What about that ten thousand nicker?'

'Oh crikey, another of 'em! That's a pie everybody would like to have a finger in. What makes *you* think you'll get any of it?'

Gurk allowed himself to leer cunningly: the man who was not going to be tricked into giving an incriminating answer. 'Suppose, just suppose, Norry and me get our lot for this bank job? If the law says we done it, then the law has got to say we're entitled to our share of the crinkle.'

'Why?'

Gurk took a deep breath. 'Look,' he said. 'Spurr is claiming that money, isn't he?'

'Perhaps.'

'Right, and no perhaps about it. To do that he has to admit the job, and come copper on me and Norry so's he'll get off light. If the judge swallows that, then me and Norry get a lagging because we shared in the job. So we're entitled to share in the take.'

'Take? Do you mean the bank's money?'

'No! I mean the money the bank's money was swopped for.'

'But, guilty or not guilty, the bank's money was never yours.'

'Then it was never Spurr's either.'

'That is so.'

'So how does he come to claim the ten thousand?'

'Oh, he got that in exchange for the bank's money.'

'But he had no right to the bank's money! He stole it!'

Martineau managed to keep a straight face. 'But he isn't claiming the bank's money.'

Gurk was exasperated. He breathed through his teeth. 'Look,' he growled. 'Let's stick to the point, eh? The ten thousand nicker, and not the bank's money. What right has Spurr to have all that money?'

'None at all, except that it seems to be his.'

'Why in heaven and hell does it seem to be his?' Gurk bawled. 'He did nothing for it only sit on his arse!'

'It seems to be his because it was freely handed to him by Goosey Bright, in exchange for some stolen money.'

'In that case couldn't it still belong to Goosey? He lost the stolen money to the coppers, didn't he?'

'Yes, but that wasn't Spurr's fault. He had delivered the goods and received his pay. Goosey has no claim on that, you haven't, and Whitlow hasn't. Only Spurr has a claim.'

Gurk was outraged. 'He hasn't a shadow of right to it!'

'Morally he hasn't, but it looks as if he'll get it.'

'Well, if that's the law,' the disgusted peterman retorted, 'you can all go to hell as far as I'm concerned. I never met such a shower of crooks. Me and Norry have the most right to that money.'

'Take him away,' said Martineau.

．　　．　　．　　．　　．

Martineau was disgusted with his murder case. He had predicted that it would be a 'comic job', but it was even more 'comic' than he had expected. He had a prisoner and a reasonably sound case against him, with word-perfect witnesses. He could have been working to make it a stronger case, but because the whole thing stank of perjury he was working to upset it. It was the reverse of normal detective work, and he did not like it at all.

He kept his agents out, trying to tie Matt Spurr to an automatic pistol, and turned his attention to other matters. But not for long. There was a happening which caused considerable excitement and gave him a faint hope that he might acquire new evidence of the sort he wanted.

It arose out of Inspector Pearson's desire to improve on a case which most policemen would have regarded as satisfactorily cleared. Like Martineau, he believed that Goosey Bright had been little more than a 'front man' for one or more capitalists of crime. He wondered if further questioning of Matt Spurr would produce some revealing remark which might lead to further investigation. He sent for Matt.

Five minutes later there was an incident which was the cause of hilarity among lower ranks of the force who were in no way involved. A young C.I.D. man and a comparatively elderly gaoler escorted Matt from his cell. They did not expect to have any trouble. Spurr was a quiet prisoner who, they had heard, would be pleading guilty and betraying every accomplice in sight. Certainly they held him after a fashion, but it was a matter of two men each thinking that the other had a firm hold of the prisoner, when in fact neither had more than two fingers on his arm. They came out of the cell corridor in this manner, never dreaming of disaster, and Matt saw his opportunity, broke away, and ran straight out of the building. He was pursued by the C.I.D. man, the constable on duty at the door, and – lying third and losing ground all the time – the gaoler. As luck had it there was no police vehicle near the front door at the time, and the only traffic in sight was a loaded three-ton lorry, accelerating away from a corner. Matt was able to reach the lorry and grasp one of the ropes which held the load. As the lorry went faster he ran with giant strides, and when at last he had to let go the pursuing policemen were far behind and out of breath. He ran into the warren of streets which was the financial section of the city, and got away.

With regard to his escape, the story went round the force that while he was in the police station he had marched along in step with his escort, marked time two paces, smartly turned about, and bolted while his escort went marching on. There was no humour in the story for the gaoler, who was afterwards reprimanded for neglect of duty, and the C.I.D. man, who suffered for his carelessness by being returned to street duty in uniform.

The escape was effected at ten o'clock on Thursday morning, when most of the senior officers of the force were in the police building. The news went around. Everybody was surprised, but nobody except Pearson was worried. That was to be expected. Spurr was Pearson's prisoner and main witness. Let him do the worrying.

'I've lost faith in him,' he said to Martineau. 'He's let me down. What does the silly little blighter think he's going to gain by slinging his hook?'

'I don't suppose he thought at all,' said Martineau. 'He saw a chance and took it. Now, he's probably wondering why. Regretting it, maybe.'

'He'll regret it when I get hold of him.'

'He's impetuous, irresponsible, and not too intelligent. He won't have any plans. He nipped away on the spur of the moment, I imagine. Ha ha! Spur of the moment.'

'I'm not laughing, sir. He's your witness as well as mine.'

'I wouldn't care if I never saw him again. I wonder what hole he's crept into.'

'I've staked out his home, the place where his sister works, Mavis Reeder's place, and Blascoe's Gym. And I've got every policeman in four counties looking for him. What more can I do?'

'Wait, just wait. He'll be picked up.'

'I suppose so,' said Pearson, worried just the same.

.   .   .   .   .

Bill Hearn was in the C.I.D. main office when news of the escape was brought in, and he was the first person Pearson saw when he ran out of his own office looking for men.

150

'Matt Spurr has escaped,' Pearson said. 'You go to Blascoe's Gym as quick as you can. I'll send you a mate as soon as I have a spare man.'

Bill realized that if Spurr was going straight to the gymnasium, it was important that a policeman should get there before him. 'Do I take a car, sir?' he asked.

'If there is one,' Pearson snapped. 'Off you go!'

Bill hurried out to the yard. He looked round for a C.I.D. car and saw an Area Patrol car just moving off. He ran, signalling.

'Be a pal,' he said to the uniformed driver. 'Drop me at Blascoe's Gym. I'm in a hurry.'

The A.P. car took him to Blascoe's. On the way he wondered what Sable's attitude would be if he did happen to be the one who recaptured her brother. If that occurred, there would be no possibility of future friendship, he felt sure. Sable was endowed with a full share of womanly sentiment, and this would be stronger in personal relations than any amount of logic. Arrest of Matt by Bill would be the end of something which, as yet, had hardly had the chance to begin. Bill almost hoped that he would not see Matt.

At ten minutes past ten the gymnasium had not been open for more than a few minutes. There were no customers. Bill looked into the office and found Nipper reading the sports page of his morning paper while he waited for the kettle to boil on a tiny gas ring.

He looked up from the paper and said: 'Hello. You again, is it?'

Bill considered him. He showed no sign of uneasiness or guilt. The paper in his hands was perfectly still. He did not look like a man who was hiding a fugitive.

Still watching closely, Bill said: 'Matt has given us the slip. He's escaped.'

The battered, ingenuous face showed surprise, concern, and excitement all at once. 'An' you're here lookin' for him?' he asked.

'That's right. I'm in the open, Nipper.'

'Aye. Fair enough,' Nipper replied. Then he said with a tremor of anxiety in his voice: 'He won't come here'.

'In a way I hope he doesn't. But it makes no difference where he goes. Here or some other place, he'll get picked up.'

'Happen he will. He'll have nowhere to go except where police is on the lookout for him. Where was he hidin' the first time?'

'In a furnished room,' said Bill rather shortly. He did not want to have to tell Nipper that his grandson had resided with a prostitute of the cheaper sort. 'They won't have him there again. Now, he's a man who has escaped from police custody. They won't harbour him.'

Nipper nodded. 'The poor lad might as well a-stayed where he was. Mind you, fellers *have* been known to get clear away.'

'Not fellows like Matt. With no money and no friends he hasn't a chance,' Bill said with certainty.

The kettle changed its tune as the water began to boil. Nipper made tea, and poured two cups. He handed one to Bill, and they sipped the tea in silence. It was a companionable silence, Bill thought. Nipper could not remain unfriendly with someone for whom he had an admiration, however reluctant it might be.

The outer door banged. Bill could see it from the corner where he was sitting. Nipper sprang from his stool and looked round the edge of the office door. 'It's all right,' said Bill, not moving at all.

Detective Sergeant Devery and Detective Constable Cassidy came to the office. Devery was holding a search warrant and slapping his open palm with it. He showed the warrant to Nipper, but spoke to Bill. 'You got here all right. Any sign?'

Bill shook his head. Devery nodded as if he had expected no more than that. 'You stay where you are and watch the door,' he said. 'We'll look around.'

While the brief search went on, Nipper showed no concern. It remained obvious to Bill that Matt was not on

the premises with his grandfather's connivance or permission, at any rate.

The door banged again, and every man in the place
looked to see who had arrived. It was Sable, and she had
been crying. She ran to Nipper and, with her head on his
shoulder, burst into tears anew. The old man patted her, and
had nothing to say. Bill looked on helplessly. He would
have liked to creep away unobserved, but he was im-
prisoned in the office by Sable and Nipper in the doorway.

'Matt is out,' the girl cried between sobs. 'The police are
after him again. They've been to the office seeking him.'

'There there,' said Nipper. 'There there.'

'What will they do to him? Oh, what will they do to him?'

Sergeant Devery beckoned to Bill. He tried to squeeze
past the couple in the doorway. Sable noticed him for the
first time.

'You! You came here to trap him, didn't you?' she
accused wildly. 'You came here to trap my brother.'

Clear of the doorway, Bill turned and looked at her
without answering. He could think of nothing to say.

Sergeant Devery was a good fellow and an acute ob-
server. He saw misery on Bill's face; emotion far deeper than
mere embarrassment. To him it seemed strange, but it was
unmistakable.

'Come away,' he murmured to Bill. 'It's a fine day. You
can watch this place from outside.'

17

NEWS of Matt Spurr came from an unexpected source four hours after his escape. A pawnbroker in Rubber Street, the main thoroughfare of an unsavoury area, telephoned Headquarters and asked to speak to Detective Sergeant Devery. Devery was not available. 'Can I speak to Mr. Martineau, then?' the pawnbroker asked.

The call was put through to the chief inspector. He knew the pawnbroker well. 'Now then, Mr. Green. What's the trouble?' he asked.

'I didn't want to bother you about this,' Green replied. 'It's one of those things which may turn out to be nothing at all. I don't mind admitting I've been wrestling with my conscience about it. My conscience won, and now I may be talking myself out of ten pounds.'

'A clean record is worth ten pounds.'

'It is indeed. This is what happened. About half an hour ago a young fellow came in and pledged a gold hunter watch, a very good one. He said his name was Victor Eaglan. I looked at the watch and read the inscription inside the front cover. It said that the watch had been presented to Victor Eaglan in recognition of twenty-five years service as honorary secretary of Boyton Bowling Club. Well, the Eaglan in the shop didn't look twenty-five years old. He must have read my thoughts about that, because he said his father was called Victor Eaglan, too, but he was dead. I asked him if he would like to sell me the watch, but he didn't fall into the trap. He said the watch was a keepsake, and he only wanted to pledge. That made me think he was honest, and I took the watch and gave him a ticket.'

'You allowed him ten pounds on the watch?'

'Yes. A very good watch. Well, after he'd gone I thought

154

about the name Eaglan. It isn't a common name but it seemed familiar. I went through into the house and mentioned it to my missus, and she said there was an Eaglan being had up for murder. I remembered the whole thing then. I'm hoping this watch has no connexion with that particular Eaglan, but funny things happen in my business, as you know. I thought I'd better phone the police.'

'I think you did right, Mr. Green,' said Martineau. 'Look after that watch. Somebody will be coming round to look for it. Now, give me the description of the man who pledged it.'

'Twenty-three years old, happen. Smallish. Not bad looking, with rather a lot of brown hair. Clean shaven. He was wearing a brown leather jacket.'

'Thanks. Be seeing you, Mr. Green.'

Martineau telephoned the front office and passed on the information that a man answering to the description of Matt Spurr had been seen in Rubber Street at 1.30 p.m. Then he rang for a gaoler, who went with him to see Cliff Eaglan. The prisoner was lying in his cot, reading a book. When he saw Martineau, he put the book aside and sat up. A look of guarded hope appeared on his face.

'No,' said Martineau. 'I haven't come to let you out. What was your father's full name?'

'Victor Eaglan.'

'You once mentioned that you had a gold watch of his. Where should it be, now?'

'In a drawer in my room.'

'Hm. It appears to be in a pawnbroker's shop in Rubber Street. Will you describe it to me?'

Eaglan described the watch, and quoted the inscription.

'That's the one,' said Martineau. 'It's been stolen, but you'll get it back. Was there anything else of particular value in the room?'

'Of particular value? No.'

'Any money?'

'No,' said Eaglan.

Martineau returned to the C.I.D., and looked in on

Pearson. He recounted the story of the stolen watch. 'I'm away to Eaglan's lodgings now,' he concluded.

'And I'm coming with you,' said Pearson.

The two men drove to Lonsdale Road, where they interviewed Eaglan's landlady, Mrs. Burton.

'Have you been in Mr. Eaglan's room today?' Martineau asked.

There was no hesitation about the reply. 'No,' the woman said. 'I haven't been into that room since the police came and searched it and locked it up.'

'Will you show us the room now?'

'Certainly.' Mrs. Burton led the way upstairs, and pointed to a door. Pearson stooped to examine the police seal. 'This seems to be all right,' he said.

'Break it,' Martineau commanded.

The seal was broken, and Mrs. Burton unlocked the door with her own key. The three of them entered a room which was in disorder. Drawers had been pulled out and their contents scattered. Bedclothes were on the floor. The mattress had been ripped. Articles of furniture had been moved away from the wall.

The room was cooled by a pleasant breeze from the open window. 'He got in the same way as his sister,' Martineau remarked.

'What could he hope to find, apart from something to flog?' Pearson wanted to know.

'The lad is simple. I expect he was looking for some clue to the crinkle. A safe-deposit key, maybe. What a hope!'

They left the room and locked the door. As they went out to their car Martineau said: 'So all we know is that young Spurr has ten pounds. That would take him quite a long way.'

'It won't take him anywhere,' Pearson stoutly affirmed, but he looked unhappy. Matt could have travelled more than a few miles between the time he left the pawnshop and the raising of the alarm.

The two men went to Rubber Street and collected Eaglan's watch and a statement from the pawnbroker.

From there they rode in heavy traffic through the heart of the city. Pearson concentrated on driving the car, and Martineau was able to meditate undisturbed. He did not waste time by pondering what he would do if he were in Matt's predicament, because that young man's mental processes – if any – were widely disparate from his own. Instead, he studied facts and assumptions, and he put a question mark to one of these latter. There was no real basis for the theory that Matt had no friends who would shelter him. If, as Martineau believed, there was a conspiracy to clear Matt of suspicion of murder by inculpating Cliff Eaglan, then Matt had at least one friend, and that one a man of power.

At this point in his cogitations Martineau substituted the word 'accomplice' for 'friend', because the man he had in mind was no other man's real friend. There was a profit motive somewhere. The chief inspector sought for this in the light of what he believed. Matt Spurr had been betrayed to the police by a person who preferred to remain anonymous. The betrayal itself had probably been a faked job. Matt and Goosey Bright had had their stories ready, and they had named their witnesses without hesitation. Also, Matt had had no hesitation in putting the finger on Gurk and Whitlow. Matt was to be cleared of murder, and he was working for a shorter sentence by 'giving every assistance to the police'. So far, the puzzle could be assembled nicely, but one or two pieces were missing. How was the man behind the conspiracy going to be able to relieve Matt of ten thousand pounds while he was in prison? He was not the sort of man to wait two or three years for money which he would regard as his own. How would he view the matter of Matt's escape? Surely such an action was contrary to his plans? Was Matt still busily trying to double-cross everybody, as he had tried all along?

Would Matt, hard pressed and with nowhere to go, finally go to the head of the conspiracy, Dixie Costello? Martineau tried hard, but he failed to think of any reason why the fugitive would do that. Then he remembered that

Matt did not seem to be guided by reason in some of his actions. He *might* go to Costello.

Here Martineau sighed. Of all places in town, Costello's flat was the most difficult from the point of view of police observations. Attempts to watch the flat invariably ended in Dixie knowing all about them in a matter of hours. Dixie found it worth his while to be a good neighbour and occasionally a benefactor in All Saints Road. Many of the people in the vicinity genuinely liked him, and none of them wanted to take the risk of being known as a main or contributory cause of misfortune to him. As a result, the police could not go near the flat without Dixie learning of their presence.

At Headquarters, Martineau sat in his office and thought about the man whom he had been trying to snare for twenty years. He looked at his watch. At that time in the afternoon it was quite probable that Dixie would be sleeping off the effects of the lunch-time liquor. Awakened from slumber by a telephone call, he might be caught off his guard, or at least be slightly less alert than usual. In any case it would be interesting to find out, eventually, whether or not a piece of information would induce him to make some revealing move.

The chief inspector picked up one of his three telephones. It was the one which was not connected with the police switchboard. He dialled Costello's number. He had known the number for years.

He waited. The whirr of the telephone stopped. There was a woman's voice. 'Hello.'

'This is Chief Inspector Martineau,' the policeman said. 'I want to talk to Mr. Costello.'

'It's one of the top coppers, dearie,' he heard the girl say. 'Have we time to bother with him?'

There was a pause, and then the girl said: 'Martineau.' A longer pause, and then Dixie said: 'What do you want, Martineau?'

'I want to tell you that a lad called Matt Spurr has escaped from police custody.'

158

Dixie yawned. 'Good luck to him. Why tell me about him?'

'Your boys can usually get the griff. I'd appreciate any news of Spurr.'

'Oh, you would, would you? You know very well the grasshopper lark is against my principles.'

'Principles? You haven't got any.'

'How little you know. You won't get me turning anybody in. If you want this Spurr, catch him yourself.'

'Thanks, I probably will,' said Martineau, and he put down the receiver. With a rueful grin he mused: 'When you catch a weasel asleep, whistle in his ear.' He also thought: 'Now, we'll see if anything happens.'

. . . . .

After receiving an urgent summons and an angry command from his chief, Ned Higgs deployed all his available manpower in the search for Matt Spurr. He was confident that he would find the fugitive, and his confidence was based on experience. He had sources of information which were closed to the police. Detectives entering low-class resorts were always expected to be looking for somebody or some thing, and their most casual questions were treated with suspicion. For information from such places they usually had to depend on 'grass', and purveyors of this were few in number. Members of the Costello mob were under no such handicap. Nobody expected them to be hunting anyone. They could learn what they wanted to know simply by appearing to pass on the gossip of the day, and they could converse freely with people who would not open their mouths to the police. If Matt Spurr was still in Granchester he would have to show his face sooner or later. When he did that, Ned Higgs would be told.

Spurr had a comparative freedom of movement until the normal editions of the evening newspapers appeared on the streets. Before that happened, he had a chance to find a friend and a hiding place. Higgs received his orders shortly after three o'clock, when all the licensed houses in the city had closed for the afternoon. So, in the beginning, his men sought news of Matt Spurr in clubs and cafés. But when the pubs reopened at half past five they were ready, and before six o'clock they were on his trail.

It was the man known as Waddy who picked up the scent. His second calling place after five-thirty was an inn with the sign of The Prodigal Son. The licence was held by a widow called Hannah Savage. But she was old and feeble, and the inn was managed by her forty-year-old son, Douglas, who could not hold the licence himself because of his police record. Doug Savage's record included two cases of larceny-bailee from his own mother. His friends did not despise him for these crimes, because they were regarded as 'unintentional'. He had simply gone to the races with the inn's takings, and lost the lot. Well, he might have won, mightn't he?

The Costello crowd had never crossed Doug's path, nor he theirs. Some of them were customers of his, and wary friendliness was his feeling for them. There were only half a dozen people in his bar when Waddy walked in, and he was not busy. He greeted the newcomer with a grin, served him with a whisky, and pushed forward the water jug. 'I'm a right sucker,' he said.

'I know that,' said Waddy with mild humour. 'But what makes *you* realize it?'

Doug nodded towards an evening paper which was spread on an unoccupied part of the bar. 'This Spurr laddie who walked away from the coppers. He kidded me.'

Waddy showed surprise. 'He did? You let him bite your ear?'

'No fear. They don't touch me for money. But he kidded me all the same.'

'Has he been in here?'

Doug nodded solemnly. 'Between two and three. I knew who he was. I said: "I thought they had you locked up". He never turned a hair. Said he was out on bail.'

'Boy, you were kidded.'

160

'You're wise after the event. He was sitting there, at that table, and he had money. What else could I think?'

'He had money?'

'Yes, a little wad. I said: "How come they let you have bail?" and he winked and said: "I've got big people behind me". Well, he did have at that. A crowd of coppers.'

'Was he on his Tod?' Waddy wanted to know.

'He was when he came in. But he went and sat aside of Half-crown Annie, and he was soon talking to her.'

'Buy her a drink, did he?'

'Three or four. The old cow was in clover. He bought a couple bottles gin just before closing time and went out with her.'

'Mmmm.' Waddy did not seem to be greatly interested. 'Where's Annie living these days?'

'You mean what dustbin does she crawl into at night? Blest if I could tell you. I don't let her come in here as a rule. Peggy served her when I wasn't looking. I was going to see her off after the first one, but when young Spurr started buying 'em I thought I'd give the old girl a break.'

Waddy wanted to get away from there, but he did not want to show any sign of haste. 'You weren't giving the boy much of a break,' he said.

'Oh, there's no fool like a young fool. I say let 'em learn. That kid is a natural low-lifer, anyway. Half-crown Annie. Ugh!'

'You're making me sick,' said Waddy. He finished his whisky and walked out of the inn. Three minutes later he was in a public telephone box, dialling a number.

As a result of the phone call, the Costello organization was given the task of locating the habitation of Annie Richmond, who had once been a lady and was now the cheapest of drabs. The cheapest, but not the meanest. An old prostitute who, these days, very rarely succeeded in finding a man willing to dally with her, she would accept drinks, tips, garbage, scraps, kicks, anything. But she would not steal and she would not tell a lie. This strangeness in Annie was well known in the compact heart of the big city of Granchester, where people in all walks of life, from financiers to flower sellers, were apt to be acquainted with each other. Dixie Costello knew all about it. 'Make sure Annie sees nothing,' he ordered. 'If she knows anything, smothering is the only way to stop her from telling the truth.'

Daylight had fled before Ned Higgs found out where Annie was living. She had one room at the end of a row of condemned dwelling-houses. Half the row had been demolished, but Annie's house would be the last one to feel the shock of the bulldozer. Higgs estimated that she would have possibly another week of free tenancy before she was compelled to find another shelter.

He went with William (The Dog) Wolfe, Waddy, and a man called Sammy Orpington to get Matt. While Waddy and Orpington acted as lookouts, he and Wolfe went towards the house. There was a dim light in a room on the ground floor, and the single window had a curtain of sacking. At the top of the window the sack sagged, and in the middle there were four inches of uncurtained glass above it. The stone window sill was high, nearly five feet above street level. Higgs reflected that if Matt were in the room he would feel secure from observation.

He nudged Wolfe, and pointed first at the window sill, and then at the top of the window. 'Lift me up, gently,' he whispered. The huge man nodded, picked him up, and carefully placed his heels on the edge of the window sill. Then slowly with a great hand moving down from shoulders to hips he was pushed into an upright position. He steadied himself with a hand on the brickwork beside the window, and looked down into the room.

The light in the room was one candle-power, and the candle was stuck in the neck of a small beer bottle which stood on the shelf of the fireplace. In the centre of the room there was an overturned tea chest which served as a table. Matt and Annie were seated beside it on smaller boxes. On the table was a gin bottle and two cups of different shapes. Another bottle stood on the fireplace beside the home-made candlestick. In the far corner of the room a mattress lay on the floor. Higgs knew that the mattress was Annie's only article of furniture. She rolled it into a bundle and carried it with her when she moved from one makeshift home to another.

Annie sat directly facing the window, and Matt showed his profile to it. As Higgs watched, the woman reached for the bottle and unsteadily poured some gin into Matt's cup, and then refilled her own. She raised her cup and made some remark, and her friendly smile was a drunken leer. Smiling faintly, Matt raised his own cup and put it to his lips. Annie took a deep drink of the neat gin and made some remark which she found extremely amusing. Her bout of laughter ended in a fit of coughing. Matt watched her impassively.

Higgs made a signal to Wolfe, and the big man lifted him down from the window. They tiptoed away, then strolled a short distance. 'We'll have to wait a while,' said Higgs. He lit a cigarette, and looked up at the sky. 'A lovely night,' he commented. 'This has been the best April we've had in years.'

They smoked and talked in low voices for half an hour, then Higgs was put on the window sill again. He looked into the room. Annie lay sprawled on the mattress. Her mouth was open and her eyes were closed. Matt was sitting at the 'table', brooding.

Higgs had himself lifted down. 'Right,' he whispered. 'We'll cover up, in case Annie wakes. We don't want to have to do her in.'

They tied handkerchiefs to cover their faces up to the eyes, and then they pulled on soft leather gloves. Higgs went to the door and tried it gently. It was locked. He raised the letter-box and spoke through it.

'Matt,' he hissed. 'Matt. Let me in.'

Matt was at the door in an instant. 'Who is it?'

'It's me, Ned Higgs,' came the insistent whisper. 'You've got to move. The cops'll be here in five minutes.'

Matt opened the door, and then he tried to close it when

he saw the mask. Higgs pushed him back into the room, and entered. Wolfe followed, and closed the door.

'You can forget that bit about coppers,' Higgs remarked. 'That was a gag. But from here on I'm talking serious.'

Matt stood white-faced, in speechless apprehension. Wolfe calmly moved the bottle and the two cups from the tea chest to the fireplace, then he moved the chest and the two smaller boxes to the side of the room.

'You didn't listen proper when I talked to you before,' Higgs went on. 'Now I'm going to make sure you remember every word. You're going to remember every word, but you're not going to mention my name to anybody, see? What did you run away from the coppers for?'

'No reason particular. I saw a chance and took it.'

'You still had it in your crackpot head you could diddle everybody and clear off with that ten thousand, didn't you?' Higgs said. 'That's the silliest idea I ever heard of. From now on you'll do as you're told, and say what you've been told to say.' His tone changed slightly as he went on: 'Don't mark his face at all.'

That was a signal to Wolfe. He moved and grasped Matt by the shoulder, turning him. He transferred his grip to the back of Matt's neck, where he got a firm hold on the collar of the leather jacket. With his free hand he delivered a kidney punch. Matt gasped in agony and arched away, whereupon Higgs, standing in front of him, hit him hard in the stomach. Then the two mobsters sychronized their efforts. Matt was held dangling while he received simultaneous blows from in front and behind. He made no sound other than the gasps and grunts of a man fighting for breath. After a while Higgs said: 'Drop him,' and he was lowered to the floor. 'Get the car,' was the next command, and Wolfe departed. Higgs went to look at Annie, and saw that she was still asleep. He returned to the helpless man on the floor and passed the time of waiting by kicking him in the ribs.

Wolfe returned and picked up Matt, and carried him out to the car. Higgs took a final look at Annie, then he blew out the candle before he left the room. As the car went slowly along byways Matt revived. When it was being driven under the bright lights of the city's centre he was able to sit up unaided, though the effort was obviously painful.

'Where you taking me?' he muttered.

'You'll know in a minute,' Higgs replied.

A minute later the car stopped a hundred yards away from Police Headquarters, on the opposite side of the street. Higgs reached into the cubby-hole of the car and brought out a flat half-bottle of gin. 'Have a drink,' he said.

Matt took the bottle and tried to take a long swig. He could not raise his arm high enough. Higgs reached, and held the bottle for him, and when he took it away he spilled a liberal amount of the spirit on Matt's shirt and tie. 'Now then,' he said. 'Do you know where you are?'

Matt peered out through the windows. 'Police station,' he said thickly.

'Yeh. That's where you're going, and you're walking the the rest of the way. Go on, get out!'

Somebody opened the door nearest to Matt. Painfully he climbed out of the car. 'And this time don't forget what you been told,' said Higgs before the door was slammed.

Matt crossed the road and walked slowly and unsteadily towards the public entrance of the police station, and the car moved along abreast of him. He entered, and the car put on speed, but stopped again about sixty yards away. Higgs looked at his watch. He allowed three minutes to pass. He said: 'He won't come out now. Let's go.'

.   .   .   .   .

Martineau went into the charge room when he heard that Matt Spurr had surrendered of his own free will. He found Pearson already there, watching a gaoler search the prisoner.

'We won't be able to talk to him tonight,' said the inspector in disgust. 'He's pickled to the eyes.'

'He looks sick,' said Martineau.

165

'Sick drunk. I expect he's been puking all over the place.'

The busy gaoler thrust his big hand inside the front of the leather jacket. Martineau saw Matt wince. 'Get that jacket off,' he ordered. 'And the shirt.'

Matt did not object as he was stripped to the waist. His body up to the shoulder blades was red, pink, black and purple. Pearson ordered the police surgeon to be called.

'How did you collect this lot?' he asked.

'Got into a fight,' Matt mumbled. 'Irishman.'

'What Irishman? What was his name?'

'Don't know. Never saw him before.'

'Where did this happen?'

'Outside some pub or other. Can't remember.'

'What time?'

'Hour ago, happen. I dunno.'

'You kept your face out of the way, I see.'

'Guarded m' face. Never touched it.'

'You're lying, aren't you?'

'You'll never know.'

Martineau turned away. He knew. He had seen the results of mobsters' punitive expeditions before. Until that moment he had had strong suspicions about Dixie Costello's involvement in what was now known as the Kaplan and Ray (Eaglan) murder case. No longer did he merely suspect, he was certain.

He also had the answer to a question which had been puzzling him. How did Costello expect to be able to compel Matt to do his bidding while he was in prison? Martineau could not yet perceive precisely what method would be used to bamboozle the prison authorities into the belief that Matt's money was being transferred in a normal way, but he knew that there would be extortion, and he knew how Matt would be made to submit to it.

'Not on your life, Dixie,' he said to himself. 'I'll stop your little caper.'

166

18

ON Saturday morning the 2nd May, Cliff Eaglan, Matt Spurr, Norry Whitlow and Grubber Gurk again appeared before the Stipendiary Magistrate. In Eaglan's case Chief Superintendent Clay again asked for a remand in custody. In doing this he was following the wishes of a subordinate, because Martineau was playing for time and still hoping to find evidence which would point definitely to the real culprit, whether it were Eaglan or Spurr. A remand of six days was granted, and Eaglan was taken below to await transport to Farways Gaol. In England a prisoner cannot be kept in police-station cells for longer than four days.

Sitting in the courtroom Martineau followed his usual habit of looking round to see who might be in the public gallery. The habit had been rewarding in the past. The sight of a certain person listening to the evidence in a certain case can sometimes start a detective on a new train of inquiry.

In this instance Martineau was not at all surprised to see Ned Higgs among the crowd in the gallery. Dixie Costello would not demean himself by sitting among the odds and ends of humanity who were the usual spectators in a magistrate's court, but he was interested enough to send his most trusted and intelligent henchman.

Once more the three men involved in the Northern Counties Bank robbery climbed the steps to the dock, and again they were heavily guarded. This time Clay did not ask for a remand. Pearson had completed his case, and he had ample evidence to support the statement of Matt Spurr. Depositions were taken, Spurr, Whitlow and Gurk reserved their defences, and were remanded in custody until the next Crown Court of Assize in Granchester. The

Stipendiary did not quite laugh at their legal representatives' solemn application for bail, and the equally solemn police opposition to the application. The three were taken below, where they also awaited transport to Farways.

They did not have long to wait. With Eaglan and their escort they made up a full load for a prison van. They were not taken back to the cells, but ushered into the charge room. There was some delay while the preliminaries of transfer to prison were completed, and during this time the atmosphere of hatred was almost tangible. The policemen in the room were aware of it, and when Gurk did suddenly try to close with Matt his swinging blows were blocked and he was dragged away from his betrayer. Whitlow watched the incident with a faint curl of contempt on his lips. A black eye or a bloody nose for Matt was not his idea of vengeance.

When the 'consignment notes' and other necessary documents were completed, the gaoler turned to a table where there were four little heaps of bright steel. These were the strong chains with which the prisoners would be manacled to the body of the prison van. Each length of chain was some eighteen inches long, with a heavy steel ring at each end. One of the rings was a handcuff and the other, the heavier one, was made to slide on an inch-thick bar inside the van. The gaoler locked a handcuff on each prisoner's right wrist, always keeping hold of the chain until a policeman of the escort had grasped the ring at the other end. Then the party filed out into the police station yard, where the van was waiting.

The interior of the van had four seats on each side, and each seat was separated from its neighbour by a wooden partition which was as deep as the seat and as high as the ceiling of the van. Along the backs of the seats, low down, ran the van bars. They were strongly held by a wide bracket at each seat, and a socket for the bar ran through each bracket. Four adjacent seats were allotted to the prisoners, and there was a click as the driver pulled back a lever to open the van bar behind their seats. Near the bracket behind each seat there appeared a break in the bar.

The solid ring at the end of each man's chain was slid on to the bar.

'Right-o,' one of the policemen called.

The driver pushed forward the lever, and the gaps in the bar were no longer visible, being inside the brackets. The prisoners were secured to the body of the van and the only man who could release them was out of their reach, in the driver's cab.

The four policemen of the escort sat down facing the prisoners, and one of them locked the door and put the key in his pocket. Another policeman knocked twice on the back of the driver's cab, and the van set off on its short journey to the prison. The driver had traversed the route hundreds of times. Apart from the fact that his passengers were exceptionally well guarded on this occasion, it was just an ordinary trip to him.

The heavy forenoon traffic in the middle of the city made it a slow journey at first, but soon the van was passing through the inner suburb of Shirwell, where the traffic was comparatively light. Common Lane was traversed at the maximum legal speed. On one side of the road was Shirwell Common, a half-mile square of land which was a recreation ground for children and on the other side were rows of small terrace houses. At the farther corner of the common there was a crossroads which had neither traffic lights, roundabout, nor policeman on point duty. Drivers approaching it had a clear view in all directions, and it was not a place of accidents. For two vehicles to collide at the Commons crossroads there had to be a misunderstanding.

On this Saturday morning there was a small obstruction at the crossroads. Two Post Office telephone linesmen had erected a little green tent and removed the cover from a square manhole. One of the men was standing in the manhole, with only his head and shoulders visible to passers-by. He was rubbing a joint on a lead-covered telephone cable, and he had put his burning blow-lamp near the edge of the manhole. His mate, not busy at the moment, was admiring the legs of a pretty girl who had just crossed the road.

The police driver saw the obstruction and felt that he was not concerned with it. It was on his off-side and not in his way at all. When he was nearly at the crossroads he gave his attention to a district nurse on a motor scooter on his near side. She was signalling her intention of going along Common Lane. It seemed to him only reasonable that she would wait until he was out of the way rather than steer across his bows, and he stated at the subsequent inquiry that she encouraged him to go forward by distinctly nodding to him. Nor did he tell a lie. The nurse admitted that she nodded, because being a person in uniform herself she always nodded or spoke to policemen and postmen.

That was the misunderstanding. The scooter and the van sailed into the otherwise clear crossing at a speed too great for mutual safety, and when the police driver saw what was happening he swerved violently to avoid a collision with the scooter. He headed straight for the manhole. One of the Post Office men shouted and leaped for his life, and the other ducked down out of sight. The policeman was braking hard, but the distance was too short. The nearside front wheel of the van dropped into the manhole. The van lurched, and its momentum turned it over on to its side. But as it went over the driver remembered his instructions in the event of an accident. He pulled back the lever controlling the van bars. The bars opened and remained open, and the prisoners were no longer chained to the van.

Of the people inside the van, the policemen came off worst in the accident. They were on the side which hit the ground. They received a bad knock, and they acted as cushions for the prisoners, who fell on top of them. The crash had sprung the lock of the van, and the door was open. Matt Spurr saw it, and at the same time he found that his right arm was free. He scrambled out, with no intention of further escape until he looked back and saw the burning glance of Norry Whitlow. He began to run across the common.

Whitlow also found that his right hand was free, and he

started to get out of the van. One of the policemen seized his coat. He turned to strike with his fist, and realized that he had a weapon in his hand. He shortened the chain and hammered the policeman's face and head with the steel ring. Lying on his back and unable to retaliate, the officer released the prisoner in order to protect his head with his hands. In the confusion the brief action was scarcely noticed. Gurk was fighting a policeman and cursing wildly, and everyone else was intent on escaping from the van. Eaglan was out before Whitlow, and he turned and offered a helping hand. Whitlow knocked the hand aside, looked for Matt and saw him, and ran in pursuit of him. Eaglan stared after him for a moment, then turned to the business of getting people out of the van.

The Post Office man who had leaped to safety was now on top of the van, helping the injured driver to climb out. The other G.P.O. man was trapped in the manhole, with a wheel of the van directed above him. His blow-lamp, out of his reach, still burned beside the wheel, and its flame was directed at the tyre.

When everyone was out of the van, Eaglan went to help the driver to get to the ground. As he did so the tyre burst into flame.

'My mate!' screamed the man on the van. 'He's in the manhole!'

Eaglan sat the driver in the road. He turned and kicked the blowlamp away from the burning tyre. 'Extinguisher. In the cab,' he called to the man on the van. The man threw himself flat and peered down into the cab. He found the fire extinguisher and passed it to the man on the ground.

The tyre burst and the flame increased. Eaglan played the jet of the extinguisher on it, and pink foam garlanded the wheel and dropped down into the manhole. 'For Christ's sake get me out of here,' the trapped man pleaded in a choked voice.

When the extinguisher was empty the flame was dead, but the tyre smouldered. The trapped man was coughing in a peculiarly painful way. Somebody said: 'We'll have to lift it.'

Eight men, injured and uninjured, policemen and prisoners, managed to move the van far enough to free the man below. As he was lifted, coughing and choking, out of the manhole, Eaglan turned and looked across the common. He had just realized what might happen there.

Here and there on the common, groups of boys were playing scratch games of football. In one place there was a real match, with two teams of youngsters and a school-teacher acting as referee. Away beyond these, making for the copse of trees and undergrowth which covered the far corner of the common, were two running men. Matt Spurr had had some forty or fifty yards start on Whitlow, but Matt's recent beating by Costello's men had not increased his stamina. Whitlow was now only ten yards behind him, and still gaining.

A police Area Patrol car with a crew of two arrived at the scene of the accident. 'Don't get out,' one of the escort called to the driver. He ran to get into the car. 'We've lost two prisoners,' he said, pointing to the running figures. The driver nodded, and the car set off along Common Lane to intercept the fugitives on the other side of the copse.

As Norry Whitlow chased Matt across the common, his mind was busy with a grim calculation. He had a sound general idea of the provisions of the recent Homicide Act. The premeditated murder of Matt Spurr purely for revenge, with no intent to gain and without the use of a firearm, was not a capital crime. Nobody could be hanged for it. Imprisonment for life was the maximum punishment which could be given. But by good conduct, and through the activities of do-gooders, a life sentence could be com-paratively short in modern times, and Whitlow could remember one reprieved murderer who had been released after serving only ten years. Well, with his record he expected to get about fourteen years for the Northern Counties Bank robbery. He didn't see how the judge could give a man fourteen years on top of a life sentence. That didn't make sense. The sentences would be passed, but not to run consecutively. They would run concurrently, and the longer of the two sentences would be served. As Whitlow saw it, the murder of Matt Spurr stood him at nothing. That, he thought, was true justice. After he had been robbed and betrayed by Spurr, it seemed right to him that he should have the opportunity to kill him and go unpunished.

The edge of the trees was marked by a fence which had been broken down in many places. Matt reeled towards one of the gaps, so wearied that he could scarcely put one foot in front of the other. When he heard Whitlow come pounding up behind him he turned to fight. He raised his arm and swung his chain and ring, but his blow never connected. Whitlow outreached him. With the action of a fast bowler at the end of his run, he brought his arm over at full stretch, and his steel ring descended squarely on top of Matt's head, and felled him.

With his enemy lying at his feet, Whitlow looked around. The school game had stopped. Twenty-two boys were looking in his direction, and the teacher-referee had started to trot towards him. But he was nearly three hundred yards away. Farther away than that, policemen were coming across the common. Whitlow perceived that he had plenty of time. He dragged Matt into the bushes and beat his brains out.

19

MATT SPURR was killed on Saturday morning. Chief Inspector Martineau waited until Monday morning, then he took Sergeant Devery with him to Blascoe's Gymnasium. They found Nipper Spurr in the little office. Martineau sat down on the stool in the corner, and Devery remained standing.

'It was a bad do, Nipper,' the senior detective said. 'I'm sorry.'

'It seemed as if it had to be,' Nipper replied sadly. 'Matt was done in by the same bad company as got him into trouble.'

'Yes. I wish the trouble was over, but it isn't.'

'It's over for our Matt.'

'Yes, he's out of harm's way. But he left a statement that might do harm.'

'How?' There was something like a challenge in Nipper's voice.

'His statement accuses Cliff Eaglan of highway robbery and murder. It wasn't given on oath and it isn't a dying declaration, but it will probably be read in court and it'll have the same effect as evidence, and Matt can't be cross-examined.'

'So what?'

Martineau looked calmly at the old pugilist. 'So Eaglan goes under,' he said.

Nipper frowned uneasily. 'There's one thing I meant to come and see you about. It can't hurt Matt now. You sent that young copper here to ask me if I'd ever seen Matt with a gun. I said I hadn't. That was true, but it wasn't the whole truth. I did see a gun in his drawer. I'd spoiled my pools coupon, an' I looked in the drawer to see if Matt had sent his in. I found the gun. Automatic pistol.'

'Did you examine it?'

'Aye. It was loaded.'

'Would you know it again?'

'Sure. There were four notches on the butt.'

Martineau expelled a long breath of relief. 'Nipper,' he said. 'You've just set an innocent man free. When was it you saw the gun?'

Nipper pondered. 'Pools night, that'd be Thursday. About half-past nine on the Thursday before the shootin' in Burleigh Street. I meant to have a word wi' Matt about it, when Sable weren't there. But I just couldn't catch him on his own, till it was too late.'

'Now I'd better go and ask Sable if *she* saw the gun. She might have wanted to protect Matt.'

'I don't think you'd better bother her. She's tryin' to forget the whole thing. She never saw the gun. I ast her.'

'Did you tell her you'd seen it?'

'No. She'd a-made me tell the truth about it.'

'In that case I'd better stay away from her,' said Martineau, with just a shade of regret in his voice. Nipper's words, and his own impression of Sable's character, convinced him that she had been telling the truth about the gun from the start. There was no need for him to distress her by going to see her about it. But, now that his anxiety about Cliff Eaglan's position was dispelled, he was as curious as anybody about the ultimate disposal of the ten thousand pounds which lay in safe deposit. It was reasonable to suppose that Sable would inherit that tainted money. To do so she would have to lay claim to it, because it was still found property in the care of the finder. He had no more idea of her intentions than anyone else, but he was one of the men most frequently asked about them. He would not have given information to merely curious inquirers in any case, but he was a little nettled by not having a valuable opinion to keep to himself.

Wondering if Nipper knew anything, he remarked:

'Sable will probably have a decision to make, about some money.'

The old man brightened. 'I've kept thinkin' it should be hers,' he said.

'What does she think?'

'I don't know. She hasn't said a word, an' I haven't liked to mention it.'

That ended the questioning. When Nipper's statement was written and signed, Martineau went away knowing that his murder case was not only cleared, it was wrapped up ready for filing. There would be no murder trial. The combined evidence of Nipper and Eaglan, two men with no police record, outweighed the testimony of crooks like Matt Spurr, Goosey Bright, and Barney Slatters. Matt was the murderer and he was dead. The case was closed.

Since there would be no trial, there would be no charges of perjury against Goosey and Slatters. Their statements had not been given on oath. If the statements did happen to be mentioned in court during the bank robbery trial, they would retract. With Matt dead there was no purpose in lying on his behalf. They would not take the risk of a perjury charge for nothing.

The bank job had been satisfactorily cleared, but there was one aspect of the subsequent receiving case which made it imperfect. It was as plain as the nose on Martineau's face that Dixie Costello had put up the whole or part of the money. But there was no evidence against Dixie. And in any case it was Pearson's job.

.   .   .   .   .

Martineau's curiosity about Sable Spurr went unsatisfied for six days after her brother's death. There had been no claim to the ten thousand pounds. Nobody had had a chance or an excuse to approach Sable. Nobody knew anything.

That bright, ambitious young man Sergeant Devery was even more curious than his 'governor'. He applied his mind to the problem of finding a reason for an official visit to

Sable, and eventually he thought of a small matter which might have been overlooked. He went to see the gaoler on duty.

'What happened to Matt Spurr's personal property?' he asked. 'Was it handed to his relations?'

'I haven't the faintest idea,' the gaoler said, with all the freedom from care of the elder policeman who has got his time in and secured his pension. He reached for the Prisoners' Property Book. He opened it and said: 'It's cancelled here. Signed by Frank Bailey when he took Spurr to Farways, the day he was killed.'

'It would be picked up after the accident,' Devery surmised.

'Very likely. C Div. would get it. They gave it to Spurr's sister after the inquest, no doubt.'

Devery hoped not, but he did not say anything. He went out of the building and requisitioned a C.I.D. car, and drove out to Shirwell where the Headquarters of C Division was situated. He entered the station and sought the gaoler, his manner brisk and important.

'Matt Spurr's personal property,' he said. 'Where is it?'

'Gone to the relations, I expect,' the gaoler said. He reached for his own P.P. book, then he made an observation concerning a fact which even Devery had overlooked. 'It can't be entered here. Spurr wasn't a prisoner in this div. He was a dead 'un. Coroner's Office is your man.'

Devery went in search of the Warrant Officer, the sergeant who also doubled as Coroner's Officer for the division. He found him in his little office, with the plain-clothes man who was his assistant. They were stooping over a Sudden Death report.

Both men looked up as Devery entered. 'If it isn't Mr. Martineau's glamour boy,' the sergeant said. 'What do you want?'

'What happened to Matt Spurr's personal property?' came the terse rejoinder.

'It went back—' began the sergeant, and he stopped and glared accusingly at his assistant. The sergeant was responsible for all work done or not done in his department, but at least he could blame his constable for not reminding him. He opened a drawer of his desk, and there was a draw-string bag and nothing else.

'Look,' he said. 'There's nothing wrong. We've been as busy as hell, that's all, and it got forgot. Who's inquiring about this?'

Devery began to hum a hymn tune for which the men of C Division had a strong dislike. Policemen of other divisions called it 'For those in peril on the C'.

'It's only Chief Superintendent Clay who wants to know, that's all,' he lied in a dry tone. 'I'd better take it now and sign for it. I might be able to square it for you.'

The Coroner's Officer was anxious. 'Do you think I ought to ring Clay and explain?' he asked.

'Sure, if you want to talk yourself into a lot of trouble. You know what he is. If I take the bag to Spurr's people, and go back and tell him they've got it, he'll ask no questions. But if you start weighing in with a lot of excuses when he doesn't know there's anything wrong . . .' Devery shrugged.

'I'll leave it to you,' said the sergeant hastily. 'Here, sign for it. Let me have the bag back sometime.'

Devery checked the property, signed for it, and departed gleefully. It was a small thing he had achieved, but it gave him pleasure. 'A bit of kiddology now and again keeps you in training,' he told himself.

Back at Headquarters he sought Martineau, and laid the bag on his desk. 'What's this?' the chief inspector asked.

'Matt Spurr's personal property, sir. C Div. still had it. I signed for it.'

Martineau looked up into his subordinate's face, and perceived his whole design. 'Let's see, it's Friday,' he mused. 'Sable will probably be at her work until about half past five. We'll go and see her after tea.'

· · · · ·

Bill Hearn had been returned to uniform duty in his own division, with an assurance from Martineau that an application for a regular trial in the C.I.D. would not be viewed with disfavour. He was Early Turn, and as he paced his suburban beat he had plenty of time to think about Sable Spurr. He was still just as anxious to know the girl better. Physically she was his ideal, and what he had learned of her character and abilities filled him with admiration. It had been love at first sight with him, and her apparent failure to have any kindly feelings for him did not lessen the emotion. He understood, or thought he did. She was loyal to her brother. Who could blame a girl for that? It showed character and courage, didn't it?

Remembering the last unlucky encounter which had left his 'relations' with Sable in such a sad state, he pondered long and seriously as to what would be a decent interval before he could approach her. She had to be allowed time to get over her brother's death. How long? A week? In that time she ought to have realized that dire misfortune for Matt had been inevitable. Surely she would not now be blaming that misfortune on one humble cog in the police machine. It never occurred to Bill that the girl might not even have thought of him since Matt's death. Having her on his mind so much made him forget that his 'relations' with her consisted of a very few very brief meetings.

Friday the 8th of May was a beautiful day, an exceptional day of an exceptional Spring. Even in sooty Granchester it was heartening weather. Bill finished his tour of duty at two o'clock in the afternoon, and after a huge dinner of steak pudding he had a bath and a second shave. In his bedroom he got out a smart new suit of lightweight tweed and surveyed it critically. It was right for the day, he thought. He dressed carefully, gave his shiny brown shoes an extra rub, and then stood staring out of the window. 'All dressed up and nowhere to go,' he mused ruefully. The trouble was that he had no girl. He needed a girl. He needed one particular girl.

'She'll be working this afternoon,' he surmised. 'I'll have to wait till after tea.'

· · · · · ·

'Yes, it makes it harder for us,' Dixie Costello admitted. 'We had Matt nicely taped. Now we've got to do the job all over again.'

'How are you going to make Sable buy your dud shares?' Conk Conquest wanted to know. 'It seems to me that if you can make her shell out, you're on to something. You can work the same trick on every wealthy woman in England. There's millions in it.'

'You can lay off the sarcasm,' said Dixie tersely. 'We got a right to the money, haven't we? When the girl knows that, it'll make a difference.'

It was Friday afternoon, and the two men were sitting in Dixie's flat. While he considered the last remark, Conk helped himself to some more of his host's brandy. Every time he filled his glass, he reflected that he was getting just a little of his money back. He had long since decided that he would not get the money any other way, though he had not actually said as much to Dixie.

'It *might* make a difference if she believes you,' he said. 'But you won't be the only one who is trying to get her to part with the brass. When she's made her claim and got the money, it'll be in all the papers. She'll be like somebody who's come up on a football pool. There'll be begging letters, and all sorts of frauds wanting her to invest, and charities wanting theirs. Dozens of 'em, there'll be.'

Dixie frowned. 'Yes,' he muttered, more to himself than to his companion. 'If she don't know the story, she'll think I'm just another of 'em. And women make a hobby of not being able to understand things they don't want to know about. It'll be half the battle if I can make her see our claim is right.'

'And what's the other half of the battle?'

'Getting her to part, of course. I'll have to talk to her very careful. But if she won't see it our way I'll talk to her even more careful. About accidents. Like if somebody mistook her for somebody else and carved her face for her, or threw the acid, or broke her up with a three-ton lorry.'

'Would you do that?'

'I'd do more than that for ten thousand nicker, but I won't have to do it. When she knows the money is mine, and I'm going to have it, she won't need the full treatment. I could show her the Dog, and tell her he likes to have his fun with the girls when he can catch 'em alone in the dark.'

'I wouldn't do that to a lady dog.'

'What does it matter so long as it works? There's Nipper, too. Happen I could get at her through him.'

'Old Nipper has worked for me a long while. He's sort of an old friend of mine.'

'Oh, I wouldn't hurt Nipper. Just the threat, see?'

'Suppose she comes copper?'

'She won't. She'll be too scared. But if she does, the game's up. I can't play rough with the coppers. If he got half a chance, that bastard Martineau would come with a dozen men with clubs and break us all up for firewood. I've got to use my superior intelligence with him.'

'So when are you going to see Sable?'

Dixie thought about that. 'I was going to wait till she'd got the money, but I see that would be wrong,' he said. 'I'd better get my claim in first. The sooner the better. If I can get her on her own, I'll call and see her after tea. Half past six, happen.'

So it was arranged. At ten minutes past six a Costello man called Bert Sloan reported by telephone that Nipper was at the gymnasium, and showing no signs of imminent departure. Conk Conquest had already informed Dixie that Nipper always stayed at the gymnasium until ten o'clock on Fridays, but the boss mobster preferred to be sure. Times were not normal with the Spurr family. In the event of any sudden change in Nipper's routine, Sloan was instructed to prevent him from getting home before seven o'clock even if he had to knock him on the head.

With Nipper accounted for, Dixie drove his black 'unofficial' car to a spot not far from Rochester Street. He was there at twenty past six, with Ned Higgs sitting beside him. Also at twenty minutes past six, the man known as Waddy knocked at Sable's door and assured himself that

181

she was at home because she answered his knock. He asked her if she knew a Mr. Raymond Porteous who lived in the neighbourhood. She replied that there used to be a Mr. Porteous who lived in the next street, but she wasn't sure if he still lived there.

Waddy thanked her and withdrew. He walked along the street and around several corners until he came to the place where Dixie and Higgs were waiting. He got into the car with them.

'She's at home, and there's no smell of coppers around,' he said.

The other two got out of the car and left him in charge of it. They walked to number 30, Rochester Street and knocked. When Sable opened the door Dixie raised his immaculate grey hat and asked politely: 'Are you Miss Sable Spurr?'

The girl owned to the name, but added: 'Please, I don't want to talk to any more reporters.'

With a sixty-guinea suit covering his excellent proportions, the boss mobster was cut to the quick by the girl's mistake, but he did not wince. 'My name is Costello,' he said kindly. 'Some people call me Dixie Costello. Perhaps you have heard of me?'

A girl with a brother like Matt and a grandparent like Nipper had certainly heard about Dixie Costello. She nodded. 'Yes.'

'I'd like to talk to you. About business. Could I come in?'

Sable hesitated. Dixie stepped forward and gently pushed her into the house, with the thought in his mind that he might as well start his acquaintance with the girl in the way that he intended it to go on. Higgs followed and closed the door. To any watcher outside the house, it would have looked as if the two men had been invited to enter.

Dixie pushed his way into the house so easily and masterfully that Sable uttered no word of protest. Nor was she apprehensive at first. She thought that her visitors were cheeky and presumptuous, but that was to be expected because they were Dixie Costello and one of his men.

Nevertheless, when she had retreated into the living room she stood with the dining table between herself and the two men, and she was within reach of the door which led to the kitchen and the backyard.

That was all right with Dixie. He looked Sable up and down, and liked what he saw. She was a redhead, and redheads were his sort of girl. He freely admitted to himself that if this had been merely a social visit he might have been willing to give her a roll in the hay. But this was business. Ten thousand pounds' worth. All he wanted was to talk to the girl, with no other witness than Higgs.

'What do you want?' she asked, embarrassed by his bold scrutiny.

'As I said, just a talk,' Dixie replied, producing his platinum cigarette case and looking for a chair. 'May I sit down?' He sat down near the table, and Higgs also found a chair.

Sable remained standing. 'Will you tell me why you have come here?'

Dixie offered his case across the table. 'Have a cigarette. The best you can buy.'

Sable shook her head, and waited. Now, her attitude was stiffly uncompromising. She did not like Costello, and she was beginning to be afraid of him.

'I'm sorry about Matt,' Dixie began. 'He was a friend of mine. He wouldn't have got into trouble if he'd listened to me.'

He looked up as if he expected some comment. When none came, he went on: 'I was helping him, you know. I paid for his lawyer. We had a verbal agreement. When he got that ten thousand pounds he was going to return it to its rightful owners.'

'And you expect me to do the same, if I get the money?'

'Yes, I do. But you'll get Matt's percentage, of course. You won't be left empty-handed.'

'You expect me to give you money, just like that?'

Dixie shook his head. 'You won't give *me* anything. And

183

it won't be just like that. It'll be arranged in a certain way, legal.'

'I'm afraid it won't be arranged with me. The money won't come to me.'

'Oh. Who gets it then, Nipper?'

'No. It won't go to him, either.'

Dixie grinned. He turned to Higgs. 'I do believe she's trying to kid me,' he said.

'I'm not kidding,' said Sable. Her fear had gone. When these men found that they would have to look elsewhere for their money, they would go away. She turned to the sideboard and picked up a letter. She held it out to Dixie. 'Read this,' she said.

Dixie's eyes narrowed. He took the letter. When he opened the single sheet of excellent notepaper and saw the letterhead of the Imperial Cancer Research Fund he bared his teeth in a grimace of surprise and shock. His face was set in that way while he read the letter, but he read it carefully. It was addressed to Sable, and it began with very proper words of consolation over her bereavement. After that it became very properly grateful, in its formal acceptance of the gift of all Sable's rights and claims to the ten thousand pounds which she presumed to have been her brother's. The Fund, the letter affirmed, would take the necessary steps to claim the money, in the interests of the cancer sufferers of the whole world.

Dixie read as far as the signature, then he allowed the letter to fall from his fingers. His expression changed. He stared straight ahead with unfocused eyes, eyes which were filled with stupefaction and horror. He could scarcely believe that this had happened to him. This stupid ninny had given away ten thousand pounds which did not belong to her. She had given away Dixie Costello's money, and put it as far out of his reach as if it were in the vaults of the Bank of England.

Fury replaced stupefied horror. Dixie looked at Sable, and when she saw his face she screamed. There was blood in his eyes. He had not been so murderously angry in years. The cut-throat in him was revealed. In speechless rage he sprang to his feet and went round the table, in time to catch Sable as she tried to escape through the door to the kitchen.

She screamed again. It was high, clear, penetrating; a fine top D scream. Then she could only moan as Dixie began to deliver the sickening body punches which were only the beginnings of the punishment he intended to inflict.

Of the three people in the room only one heard the knock on the front door which came exactly one second before the first scream. Ned Higgs heard it, and he looked apprehensively in the direction whence it came. He had not locked the door behind him when he had entered, because he had thought that such an action so early in the negotiations might alarm Sable before she needed to be alarmed. When he heard the knock he had a sudden uneasy feeling that he ought to have locked the door.

Higgs was uneasy for a very brief moment, and after that he was thoroughly uncomfortable. A big, slit-eyed fellow entered the room like an explosive blast. Sable's screams had acted upon Bill Hearn like detonators on a charge of TNT. He wafted Higgs aside while his eyes sought the girl. He saw a man beating her, and he was shaken with a rage beside which Dixie's was merely a childish tantrum. He rounded the table on the other side, and seized Dixie and turned him. His big fist smote him on the nose and mouth, and ruined the nose. The punch sent the man staggering back until he fell in the fireplace. Then Bill became vaguely aware that something had hurt the side of his head. That was Higgs, doing his best to save his boss and hoping that the two of them could cope with this wild bull of a man. Higgs was a hard man and an experienced fighter, but when the man turned on him and knocked him down, and picked him up and knocked him down again, he lost all ambition to cope. He had never been hurt so much in his life, and he wanted no more of it. Instinct told him that this man would not kick him when he was down, so he indulged

185

an overwhelming inclination and stayed where he was on the floor.

Bill turned to deal further with Dixie, but that brave man had also realized that he could not cope. Half blinded by involuntary tears, his mouth working around broken teeth, he was reeling out of the room towards the open front door. He had no thought but to get away, and he did not consider his lieutenant's plight at all.

Bill pursued him. He reached him in the doorway, but only with his foot. It was a hearty, swinging clearance kick in the right place, and it propelled Dixie forward so that he landed on hands and knees out of doors. He got up and staggered away.

Regretfully Bill let the boss mobster go. He did not want to leave Sable alone with Higgs. He returned to the living room, where Higgs had ventured to raise himself to a sitting position. He looked at Sable. 'Are you hurt?' he asked.

Gazing at him wide-eyed, she shook her head. Her expression baffled him. He stooped and seized a handful of tie, shirt, and lapel, and jerked Higgs to his feet. He looked at him, and recognized him as one of the two men he had seen in the bar of the Northland Hotel.

'Are you Dixie Costello?' he asked.

Higgs tried to speak, and gave it up. He managed to shake his head.

'Just one of the mob, eh?' Bill said through his teeth. 'All right, listen. If you or your boss or any single one of you comes within a mile of Miss Spurr again, I'll start at the top and lame the lot of you. I'll make wrecks of the whole bloody crew. Does that register?'

Half strangled, Higgs achieved a nod.

'You'll pass that message to Costello?' Bill wanted to know.

Again Higgs nodded. Bill took him to the door, and pushed him out. He closed the door and went back to Sable. 'Are you sure you're all right?' he asked.

She smiled at him, and he stared in pure delight.

186

'I'm winded, and my ribs will be sore,' she said. 'But I'll be all right.'

Bill remembered his prepared speech. This was the time to deliver it. 'I had to come around and see you,' he said. 'I hope you don't mind. You see, I couldn't leave things as they were. I er, I admire you so much, and it seemed to me to be all a sort of misunderstanding. I was hoping we could be friends.'

Light danced in Sable's eyes. He really is a darling, she thought. A big, ridiculous darling. For the first time in what seemed to be many days she was relaxed and happy, and amused.

'We can be friends,' she said. 'A girl in this town needs a friend like you. Sit yourself down. Have you had your tea?'

.   .   .   .   .

Only a minute after half past six a plain C.I.D. car turned the corner into Rochester Street. Sergeant Devery was at the wheel, and Martineau was sitting beside him.

'It seems she's got a visitor already,' said Devery, looking along the street. 'Isn't that young Hearn at the door?'

'Yes,' said Martineau. 'Stop the car.'

Devery pulled in to the kerb and stopped. 'What's he after, I wonder,' he said. Then he exclaimed: 'Oy! He knocked and walked in! He must be a regular visitor.'

'I think he'll be going a-courting,' Martineau replied. 'We'll give him a minute or two to get his feet under the table.'

A brief moment later the two detectives were surprised to see a man come flying out of the doorway of number 30 and fall on his hands and knees. This person rose to his feet and began to make erratic progress towards them, on the other side of the street.

'It's Costello,' said Devery calmly. He always became calm when any sort of action started to develop.

'You're dead right it is,' said Martineau grimly. He reached for the door handle, and sat ready to open it. Costello was not going to be allowed to pass without giving

187

an explanation of his presence in Rochester Street. If there was any slight chance that the man could be booked for any offence, any offence at all, Martineau was going to make the most of it. It is said that in dealings with crooks a policeman can always afford to wait, but Martineau had waited too long, much too long, for Dixie Costello.

He saw that Dixie was holding a bloody handkerchief to his nose, and he heard Devery murmur: 'Is his face red?' Then he was out of the car, crossing the street.

He put his solid muscular bulk in Dixie's way, bringing him to a halt. He looked at the blood-smeared face and the watering eyes.

'Why, Dixie!' he cried in amazement and pleasure. 'You're crying!'

》》》 If you've enjoyed this book and would like to discover more great vintage crime and thriller titles, as well as the most exciting crime and thriller authors writing today, visit: 》》》

The Murder Room
Where Criminal Minds Meet

themurderroom.com